THE BURDEN

By: DJLord

ISBN: 979-8-34944820-1 (EPub)

ISBN: 979-8-21872558-7 (Paperback)

Printed by IngramSpark, Inc., in the United States of America.

First printing edition 2025

www.lordandledger.com

Chapter One

Ol'Slo and the Spark

Every city has a forgotten corner — red brick and rust, where the past still leans over the present like an old man watching from a window.

Narrow streets lined with two- and three-story buildings, cars jammed into both curbs, parking always a small war of its own. On the lower floors, shopfronts teetered between boarded-up decay and quiet survival: convenience stores in the bones of old grocers, smoke shops where tailor shops once stood, and coffee windows eking out a living every other block.

People walked these streets like they had for decades, grabbing the day's bread or a carton of milk, the same way their families might have done halfway across the world.

Above the shops, curtains twitched as old women watched the street below.

A teenage boy in a hoodie leaned against the wall, thumbing at his phone, the glow reflecting off his sharp cheekbones.

The air smelled of old stone, fryer grease, and the faintest trace of cigarette smoke drifting from a window above.

And like every city, this one had tried to revitalize its forgotten quarter. You could see the effort here and there — a fresh coat of paint slapped on brick, pressure-washed sidewalks, sleek signs blinking above old facades. But next door, windowpanes gaped like blackened teeth, crumbling under the weight of time.

Between graffiti-tagged walls, you could still read the ghostly outlines of names like Sloane's, est. 1844 or Brudder Moving, est. 1903, crouched under gargoyles and chipped stone cornices.

It was a patchwork cityscape, old and new stitched awkwardly together, clinging to life like the weeds pushing up through sidewalk cracks.

A man in a sharp suit strode past the corner, murmuring into his Bluetooth, sidestepping an old woman pushing a shopping cart piled with bags.

His polished shoes clicked against the uneven pavement, his frown deepening as he glanced at the crumbling facades. "God, what a dump," he muttered under his breath.

But the old woman heard. She gave a dry laugh, half a cough, half a curse, and shuffled on.

Two blocks down, the new condominiums cast a long, clean shadow over this end of town. Their owners hurried past with tight mouths, eyes fixed forward, avoiding the occasional panhandler with an instinctive flinch.

The cars mirrored the people — gleaming new sedans parked beside bruised, rusted veterans, some still chugging along thanks to sheer stubbornness.

Despite the surface tension, this clash of past and present gave the neighborhood its pulse. They called it Old Slovenia — though few, if any, descendants of the original settlers still lived within ten miles.

To the locals, it was just Ol'Slo. Say you were from Ol'Slo, and people knew exactly the mix you meant — the cars, the buildings, the mash-up of accents and histories welded into one stubbornly alive corner of the city.

On this evening, an old green Pontiac rolled slowly up the street, its dented hood glinting under a failing streetlamp.

Inside, three men sat in silence. Dimitry chewed a fingernail down to the quick. Alexei watched the street with the steady eyes of someone used to waiting. Misha cracked his knuckles slowly; the sound lost in the rumbling of the old tires on older roads.

Their dark hair was greasy, their clothes rumpled, their faces drawn with the weariness of too many days on the road.

Fast-food wrappers littered the floor; soda cups rattled in the back seat. Once, the Pontiac had been someone's pride — now it was just another skeleton in the neighborhood parade.

They didn't even notice the red light as they drifted through the next intersection, eyes fixed ahead.

In the back seat, one of the men shifted. "You sure about this, Alexei?" he asked, voice thin with nerves.
"Drive," Misha muttered from the passenger side, fingers

drumming restlessly on his knee, glancing back at Dimitry, jaw tight, eyes squinting, telling him without words to shut up.

The driver swallowed hard. "I don't like this."

Alexei began to turn, slow and sharp.

"We don't have to like it," began Misha.

That was the last thing any of them said.

A few blocks away, a dark-haired couple moved quietly through a corner store. They filled their small tote with bread, milk, a few canned goods. Nothing that would catch anyone's eye.

They kept their heads down, never raised their eyes at anyone else in the store, offered polite nods to the cashier, and stepped out, the bell above the door jingling softly behind them.

Everyone who lived within a block of this store had been here as many times as they and noticed them just as they were aware of everyone else around them.

"Did you get the matches?" Ilya whispered.

Mikael smiled faintly. "No one's burning anything, Ilya."

She had joked for years about lighting the entire stash of money on fire and having a bonfire.

Her lips pressed tight. "You're too calm."

He gave her a look, soft but firm. "And you're too loud."

On the street, the woman hesitated, glancing left and right before crossing. The man lingered just a second longer, almost overly cautious. They checked for traffic and crossed the street toward their flat.

As they opened the lower door, the woman entered. The tall man heard the screeching of tires a half a block away, the wrenching metal-on-metal crunch as a delivery truck slammed into the Pontiac. His head snapped around in time to see the world ignite.

The fireball shot skyward, billowing between the brick buildings, rattling windows for blocks. For a moment, he stood frozen, watching the bloom of flame twist upward.

Then instinct kicked in. He ducked inside the entryway, pulling the door shut behind him just as a shockwave thumped through the street.

Inside, two elderly women from the lower flat peeked from their doorway, murmuring in worry. The man offered a tight smile, murmured something reassuring, and bounded up the stairs.

"Mikael!" one of the old women called after him, her voice shaking. "Is it safe?"
"Stay inside," he called over his shoulder, a shadow of his usual charm flickering on his face. "Please."
Behind the closed door, the two women clutched each other's hands, whispering prayers in a language half-forgotten even in this neighborhood.

By the time the detectives arrived, the street was a mess of flashing lights and scorched asphalt.

Detective John Nardone had seen plenty in his twenty years on the force, but this one made even him pause.

Flames still licked at the Pontiac's blackened shell, and the firefighters were hanging back.

"That must've nailed the gas tank just right," Nardone muttered.

A firefighter nearby shook his head grimly. "That wasn't just gas, Detective. There were weapons in the back. Guns, maybe some explosives. We're lucky this didn't flatten half the block."

Nardone's partner, Detective Eva Sayers, was already speaking with a nervous older couple outside the corner store. She waved Nardone over.

"In the store when it happened," Sayers murmured to him. "Didn't see much. But…" She hesitated as the old woman started to say something before the man hushed her in sharp, rapid Slavic. Nardone's ears perked up.

"Mind telling us," Nardone said evenly, "what she was about to say?"

The old man relented after a pause, explaining in broken English that another couple — younger, dark-haired — had left the store just before the crash. They might've seen something. Nardone and Sayers exchanged a look.

"We'll need their names," Eva said softly, kneeling to the old woman's eye level.
The old woman shook her head fiercely. "No names. Bad luck."
Eva sighed, standing. "We'll find them."

The dark couple had known by the sound of the explosions that it wasn't a simple traffic accident. It hadn't been just a gas tank erupting.

There was much more to this day, and like so many before this one, they knew it was foreboding. The noose was drawing closer once again.

Back at the precinct, the flood of witness reports blurred together: loud crash, explosion, fireball. None mentioned the couple.

Two days later, Nardone closed the last file with a sigh. "Time for some old-school work." They had no contact information for the younger couple the store owners had spoken about. That might take a drive back to the neighborhood. That might take some real detective work.

"Let's go," began Nardone sarcastically, "We're going to have to go find that couple and see if they saw anything different than the other fifty eye-witnesses."

Chapter Two

Children of Leningrad

Just out of Leningrad University, Ilya, her fiancé Peter, and his best friend Mikael brimmed with dreams of a new world.

Peter had been raised in privilege. His father was part of the Soviet machine — a high-ranking banker within the Politburo's circles, the heart of Communist power.

Peter carried himself with the effortless confidence of someone who had never wanted for anything.

What no one saw—not his professors, not even Ilya—was the duplicity Peter lived with every day.

In the morning, he attended lectures on Marxist theory, submitting essays on the virtues of class struggle. At night, he typed letters on stolen Ministry stationery for his father's associates, fudging numbers to disguise misallocated funds. He didn't do it for the thrill. He did it because it taught him how the game was played.

It wasn't just books and ideals anymore. He was learning how the levers of power actually moved—how a system supposedly built on equality ran on secrets, favors, and fear.

Once, he intercepted a telex—meant for a Party official in Minsk—containing revised shipping schedules for petroleum exports. His father had asked him to shred it. Peter read it three times instead, memorizing the discrepancies in projected vs. actual output. Someone, somewhere, was siphoning oil—and Peter suddenly understood why his father had looked pale that morning.

Later that night, while his father dozed in the den, Peter quietly snapped a photo of the page using an old camera from his uncle Dmitri.

He never printed the photo. Never spoke of it. But from that moment, the seed of treason had been planted—not out of rage, but out of certainty.

There was no redemption for this system. There would be no "gentle reform." Only rot, clawing upward.

When he told Ilya months later that he wanted to hurt the regime—not just flee it—she didn't flinch.

"Then let's be precise," she said. "If we're going to hit something, let it be something they can't cover up."

Peter smiled, the same way he did when he was a boy, nodding at the right time in his father's office—only this time, the nod meant war.

There was a natural charm about him, a magnetic ease that came from a life where doors simply opened. He had never stood in a ration line, never felt the grind of scarcity that defined the lives of so many around him.

His clothes bore discreet American labels, and in a world where the government preached Soviet superiority, it was American goods that truly signaled power.

As a child, Peter had watched his father's world with quiet disapproval. At banquets and official functions, he'd stand near the marble columns, a glass of soda in hand, listening as men in dark suits whispered about oil shipments and party favors.

He had learned early to smile when spoken to, to nod at the right moments, but inside, a different current was already stirring — one that his father never noticed.

Peter's father had done everything to groom him as his heir — sending him to the best schools, hoping he'd embrace the world of finance, the inner workings of Soviet banking.

But Peter had no interest in the family legacy. Once at university, he gravitated toward the disillusioned, the thinkers, the restless souls dissatisfied with the world they were born into.

Even as a boy, Peter understood that his world wasn't like other children's.

While his friends shared cramped flats with extended family, he grew up in a tall building with marble stairs and a private elevator that always worked.

Other boys wore patched jackets in winter; his were tailored and warm, wool from somewhere west of Prague.

His father's office had a globe taller than Peter, and a wall of leather-bound books that were never opened.

Peter's earliest memory of that office was of being told to sit still while important men talked. They laughed too loudly, slapped each other's backs, and drank crystal-clear vodka poured from bottles that weren't available in stores.

His father never looked at him in those moments. Only gestured. Only nodded when Peter did what he was told.

Once, when he was ten, he had wandered in without knocking. He'd meant to ask about his school trip — some form his mother had asked him to get signed. But he walked in on his father shouting at a man in uniform. A younger officer, stiff-backed and white-knuckled.

"No. You will not take that route," his father growled, stabbing a thick finger onto a map. "You'll follow the protocol I approved. You don't think. You follow."

The officer had saluted and left. Peter hadn't dared breathe.

His father noticed him finally, still standing by the door.

"What is it, Petya?"

"I… I need this signed. For school."

His father didn't take the form. He reached for a pen, scribbled his name without reading it, and slid it back. "Do not interrupt me in here again."

That night, Peter asked his mother what his father did.

She hesitated, eyes flicking toward the ceiling like she thought someone might be listening.

"He helps manage the people who manage the money," she said. "The men who keep the country safe."

Even then, Peter understood what she meant. His father wasn't in the KGB. He didn't wear a uniform. But he was the system — part of the engine behind the curtain.

The next time Peter felt it — that churn of quiet anger — was when his uncle came to dinner.

Uncle Dmitri had been a mathematics teacher. A simple man. Proud, gentle, always carrying a chessboard in a satchel like it was a part of him. That night, he looked thin. His clothes hung loose, and he smelled of mildew and pipe smoke.

Peter's father barely acknowledged him, his own brother.

"Dmitri," he said, sipping his drink. "Still fighting the noble fight?"

"I'm still teaching."

Peter watched the flicker of disdain cross his father's face.

"There's honor in truth," Dmitri added quietly.

"There's honor in usefulness," Peter's father replied. "And the truth, my dear brother-in-law, is a luxury for men who don't carry responsibility."

Peter saw the way his uncle's jaw tightened. But he said nothing.

Later that night, Peter found his uncle smoking outside in the snow, shoulders hunched.

"Do you like chess, Petya?"

Peter nodded. "You taught me."

Dmitri smiled, soft and sad. "That's right. You remember what I told you? That the king needs the pawns to move, but the pawns don't need the king to think."

Peter never forgot that.

It was in Leningrad where he met Ilya. It was their second year — a political studies class designed, ironically, to indoctrinate them in the "greatness" of the Communist system.

Instead, it did the opposite. In comparing political systems, the course exposed the weaknesses Soviet leaders preferred to keep hidden.

Ilya and Peter sat near each other, and soon their conversations spilled beyond the classroom: long talks over coffee, late nights wandering campus, hours spent dissecting the failures of a system they were meant to serve.

"You ever think," Peter murmured one night, cigarette dangling between his fingers, "that we're just actors in their little play?"

Ilya smirked over the rim of her coffee cup. "Then let's change the script."

That was the night Mikael found them on the university steps, still talking at three a.m., the stars sharp above their heads, the cold biting at their cheeks.

Ilya was a beauty in every sense of the word — dark-haired, sharp-eyed, with a fierce intelligence that was as magnetic as her looks. She could drink most Russian men under the table and still recall every word spoken the night before.

Where others saw vodka as an escape, Ilya wielded it like a tool — sharpening her wit, loosening her tongue, without ever tipping past the point of no return. She was, Peter often said, his match in every way.

In the smoky cafes, in crowded student apartments, Ilya's laughter rang out like a challenge. She drew people to her — not just for her beauty, but for the fire in her words, the sharpness in her eyes.

"Don't bring me flowers," she once told Peter. "Bring me arguments worth having."

And then there was Mikael — the quiet third leg of their troika. He lacked Peter's charm or Ilya's fire, but he had his own steady gravity.

Mikael first saw Ilya not in a classroom, but in a narrow, smoke-filled café three blocks from the university gates. Someone had jammed a piano against the wall and draped it with a red cloth. A kettle hissed on a burner behind the bar. Outside, the wind carried sharp snow flurries that scratched at the windows like desperate fingers.

Inside, Ilya stood at the front of the room, holding a page of carbon-stained paper. She read aloud without apology or preamble.

Her voice was clear and steady.

We are not asking for fire,
We are remembering it—
And that is what frightens them most.

No one clapped when she finished. That wasn't the point. The real applause was in the silence — the held breath of people who knew they were hearing something dangerous, something true.

Mikael didn't speak to her that night.

He just watched.

She moved through the crowd with a gravity that required no permission. Not beautiful in the obvious way — not Peter's way — but magnetic, sharp-edged. Her scarf was frayed. Her boots unmatched. Her hands moved when she talked, carving out invisible arguments in the air.

Peter noticed him noticing.

"Poetry girl?" he'd said afterward, as they trudged through slush back toward the dorms.

Mikael didn't answer.

Peter had smiled. "Careful, comrade. She doesn't believe in fairy tales. Or people."

But he was wrong.

She believed in people. Just not the ones who asked for permission to matter.

It wasn't until weeks later — after a study session turned midnight walk, after a shared joke about Marx and bad coffee — that Mikael realized she had let him in.

She told him things she didn't say in public. About her brother in exile. About the time her mother hid a banned novel under the floorboards. About standing in a bread line at age nine and memorizing the smell of hopelessness.

He didn't try to comfort her.

She didn't want that.

She wanted someone who would stand beside her and see it for what it was — not tragedy, but truth.

That was the beginning.

And in many ways, it was the only thing that lasted.

Mikael's parents were teachers, which earned him a place at the university, but he never fully fit in.

Mikael was a chameleon, someone who blended into the background, was noticed little, but himself - remembered much. He was their sounding board, the one who offered quiet affirmations and, occasionally, insights no one else had thought of.

Mikael watched them both with a faint smile, content to play the quiet observer. He carried a small leather notebook everywhere, filling its pages with lines of poetry, sketches, fragments of overheard conversation.

"You're the record-keeper," Ilya teased him once. "No," Mikael had murmured, "I just like remembering things people forget."

Together, they dreamed of something bigger.

Communism, they believed, was a beautiful idea ruined by the flawed nature of man. The theory promised equality; in practice, it created a ruling class that hoarded privilege and left everyone else scraping for crumbs.

The Politburo and their families were the new aristocracy, every bit as corrupt and insulated as the Tsars their ancestors had overthrown. For the rest of the Soviet people, life was an endless grind — hours in line for bread, no hope of advancement, no dream beyond survival.

Ilya's uncle once waited six hours for shoes, only to find they'd run out by the time he reached the front.

Peter heard the story, jaw clenched, and said softly, "A system that can't make shoes doesn't deserve to last." Mikael, seated in the corner, only murmured, "Shoes or no shoes, people survive. What scares me is when they stop wanting to."

And so, over long, cold nights, fueled by vodka and frustration, a plan began to form.

Peter's heart was restless, his ideals still uncorrupted by cynicism. He didn't want money for himself — he wanted to crack the system, to take a bite out of the machinery of control.

Money was power, and if they could seize even a small piece of that power, they could make a statement. Maybe, just maybe, they could stir the people awake.

The idea evolved with every bottle: hit the system where it hurt — the money supply. Not to get rich, not to escape, but to disrupt.

Peter's father, blinded by pride, never saw the betrayal coming. Eager to groom his son, he shared far too much — shipment schedules, armored routes, flight manifests.

Peter played the dutiful heir, asking just enough questions to be convincing, just few enough not to raise alarms.

Initially, the trio planned to hit an armored car, but they quickly realized it wouldn't be enough. One small theft would barely rattle the beast. If they wanted to make history, they needed something bolder.

That's when Peter suggested the plane.

In the 1970s and 80s, Once a month, a military flight ferried tourist money — mostly American dollars — from Leningrad to Moscow, feeding the central banking system. It was a perfect target.

Peter had known Taranov for as long as he could remember. Once, Peter was told, he had been in the KGB, and the military before that. Taranov had been in the Spetnaz, the Soviet version of Special Ops, had served in Afghanistan in the beginning and been wounded – at one point told he might never walk again. He felt almost abandoned by the military machine and a government who had promised to take care of him for life.

Taranov never thought of that anymore. He had always just "been" part of this family. He drove Peter to school when he was younger, and was always around when Peter needed anything.

Taranov had been who he leaned on when his mother passed away years ago. Peter's father had withdrawn and not handled it very well at all.

Taranov had been Peter's rock.

In Kandahar, it had been children. That was what haunted him.

He remembered the briefing — insurgents hiding in a village on the western ridge. "High probability of weapons cache," they'd said. "No civilians reported." Lies, even then.

Taranov led the unit in at dusk. Smoke coiled from distant cookfires, and the first boy they saw couldn't have been older than ten. The boy didn't run — just stared with sand-cracked lips and eyes like dark glass.

The firefight lasted four minutes. Two Spetsnaz killed, five Afghan men shot dead in front of their families. A goat screamed the entire time.

Afterward, they found nothing. No weapons. No radios. Just grain sacks, a rusted truck, and the gaze of that same boy, now smeared with blood.

Back at base, the commander called it a "successful sweep."

Taranov took no joy in vodka that night. He sat alone under the awning, cradling his weapon like a question. That was when he began to think about silence — the kind a man carried in his bones.

When he finally limped home months later, wounded and hollow-eyed, the medals felt like lead. And the country he'd bled for… it had already forgotten him.

So, when Peter later spoke of betrayal and fire and message, Taranov didn't laugh.

He listened. Because some betrayals are earned.

Taranov had always been Peter's sounding board and had heard a hundred other stories and "plans" throughout the years; plans to build a large Treehouse in the forest behind their home – which was never built, plans for where he wanted to settle afterwards – on an island somewhere off the northern coast of Russia – not realizing it wasn't tropical, or plans to leave the country and never come back.

He heard all the plans of a young man as he grows and tries to find his way in the world.

When Peter finally told him about this plan, he never doubted that Taranov would keep it in their confidence. Taranov had been like a father, and then as he had grown, become almost a big brother to him.

They pulled up to the flat the store owners had described. Nardone pressed the buzzer. A man's voice, thick with accent, answered.

"Detective Nardone, city police. We'd like to ask a few questions about the accident the other day."

The door buzzed open. They climbed the stairs to find a tall, lean man waiting at the landing.

"I'm Mikael," he said, stepping back to let them in. His partner, introduced as Ilya, hovered near the kitchen.

Nardone looked around the entire flat in a trained eye, seemingly oblivious to it all, but catching every nuance of the single room.

The small apartment was clean but cramped — kitchen, table stacked with newspapers, an old couch, boxes of various shapes along one wall. No closets, Nardone noticed it all in one glance, just the open bathroom door.

"Did you see the crash?" Nardone turned to the couple and asked casually.

Mikael's English was good, though the accent remained, never leaving when you just aren't born and raised in the United States, no matter how many years you've spent here. "We had just come home. We heard it, but we saw nothing."

Behind him, Ilya murmured something, worry crossing her face. Mikael snapped, "Tika!" under his breath — quiet but sharp. Nardone caught the Russian instantly.

Eva shifted beside him; arms crossed. "You sure about that? No one running? No one strange?" Mikael smiled thinly, "Many strange people here.

Nardone let the silence stretch, watching how Mikael's fingers curled tightly around the back of a chair.

"We appreciate your time," Nardone said smoothly, cutting off Sayers as she opened her mouth. He gave her a look: not here.

Back on the street, Sayers fumed. "What the hell, John? They're hiding something."

He nodded, sliding behind the wheel. "They're Russian. When she spoke, she said, 'They're here about the money.' He told her to shut up. So yeah — they're hiding plenty."

Sayers sat back; eyes wide. "Money? Russian? How the hell do you—?"

Nardone cracked a rare, thin smile. "Because I listen, Eva. And now we know where to start."

She gave a low whistle, glancing back at the apartment. "What do you think, they're Russian Mafia?" Eva said sarcastically.
"Not yet," Nardone murmured, turning the key in the ignition. "…and let's not get them labeled that before breakfast," he responded, not giving away anything in his voice or facial expressions.

Chapter Three

Cold Coffee, Cold Truths

Nardone had been Eva Sayers' partner for seven years, and there was still so much she didn't know about him. He didn't share much — not about his past, where he'd been, or what he'd done.

To him, it was just another chapter already written, no more or less interesting than the one they were in now.

Sometimes, when they drove in silence, Eva would sneak glances at him. His profile was all hard angles softened by wear — the deep crease between his brows, the faint scar under his left eye, the way his mouth twitched like it wanted to frown even when he was calm.

She wondered sometimes if that scar had a story. She wondered a lot of things.

For many people, that kind of secrecy would have been maddening. How do you spend most of your waking hours with someone and know almost nothing about them?

But Eva had learned it wasn't about hiding dark secrets.

Nardone simply had a personal distaste for people who couldn't stop talking about themselves — and he was determined never to become that guy.

He was nondescript in almost every way — average height, average build, a face so generic that people were always sure they'd met him before.

He often joked about it, teasing friends and strangers alike: "You must've met my double — he's everywhere."

Once, at a bar after a case, a woman had approached him with a wide smile, arms open for a hug. She froze a foot away, blinking, confusion blooming across her face. "Oh God, I thought you were someone else," she'd stammered. Nardone had just grinned, lifted his glass, and said, "Happens all the time." Eva had laughed for days over that one.

But there was nothing average about Nardone's past. Raised on military bases around the world, he had spent twelve years in the service himself.

Before joining the police, he'd been in the military himself, and had worked for the NSA as a Russian linguist and analyst. He spoke German and Russian fluently, along with a bits and pieces of a handful of other languages, and harbored a deep fascination with history.

He'd spent years absorbing every detail he could about the rise and fall of the Soviet Union, especially the rumors of enormous sums of money siphoned away by insiders just before the collapse — the hidden history, the story behind the story.

Eva sometimes wondered if his fascination with Soviet history was just professional curiosity, or if it fed something deeper in him — a longing to understand why people betrayed each other, how loyalty unraveled when tested.

She'd once asked him outright, late one night in the car. He'd just given a small, wry smile and said, "History teaches, Sayers. If you're paying attention." And that was that.

That night, after dropping Eva off and grabbing a lukewarm carton of Chinese takeout, Nardone hunkered down at his apartment.

The desk lamp cast a pale circle of light over the clutter — half-empty coffee cups, scribbled notes, and a laptop glowing softly in the dark.

The internet made it easy to chase even the most obscure rumors, but the real art was in sorting the myths from the faint threads of truth, fitting the puzzle pieces together until something meaningful emerged.

He pulled open a drawer, fishing out an old notebook — leather cover, corners worn soft, pages filled with his cramped handwriting; notes from other cases, ideas that had never panned out, names circled and underlined.

He ran his finger down the list of contacts, half-tempted to call a source in D.C. But no — not yet. Not until the pieces sharpened.

His ex-wife had always hated this side of him — the relentless way his mind worked, the questions that never seemed to end.

She used to joke that he should've gone to law school so he could interrogate someone else for a living. Maybe then they'd still be married.

He hadn't meant to make her feel like a suspect; it was just who he was. His brain couldn't rest until the pieces in front of him fit into place.

And if one didn't? He couldn't help but pick at it, reshape it, examine it from every angle.

Sometimes, late at night, he wondered if she ever missed him. He never called — didn't even know if her number was the same.

But when the apartment was quiet except for the purr of his laptop, the thought slipped in like a draft under the door.

It was raining this night — the kind of slow, soaking rain that makes everything seem quieter, like the world was holding its breath.

Nardone stood at the kitchen window for a second longer as a memory flashed back, watching the rivulets track down the glass like they were racing each other to the sill.

Behind him, the house was still — the soft tick of the wall clock, the hum of the refrigerator, the silence.

In his memory he heard her before he saw her — the soft scrape of her slippers on the hardwood, the faint hitch in her breath. She was behind him now, arms crossed, leaning in the doorway like she wasn't sure if she wanted to say something or just keep walking.

"You're not really here anymore, John," she said finally. Her voice wasn't angry — just tired. Bone-tired.

He didn't turn. "I'm here."

"No. You're at work. Or you're in your head. Or you're a thousand miles away in some place I'll never get to. But you're not here."

She paused, as if weighing whether to say the next part. Then: "I think maybe you haven't been for a long time."

The truth of it stung more because it didn't come like a slap — it came like a sigh. Like something she'd already made peace with.

He turned finally; hands braced on the counter. "I don't know how to turn it off," he said quietly. "The job. The thinking. The weight."

She nodded slowly. "I know. That's the part that scares me. I used to think it was noble. That you carried it all because someone had to. But now I see… it's not just the job, is it? You need the burden. You've made a home out of it."

Silence stretched.

She stepped closer. "You don't let anyone in, John. You never did. Even when you were standing right in front of me, there was a part of you I could never reach. And I kept telling myself that if I just held on long enough, you'd open that last door. But I'm starting to think… maybe there is no door."

He didn't argue. He just stood there, feeling the years between them gather in the space of a few inches.

A moment later, she walked away. Upstairs. To sleep in the guest room again. Or maybe just to breathe.

That was two months before the divorce papers arrived. Clean. Respectful. Like everything they'd built — quiet and orderly even in the falling apart.

He'd signed them in silence. Just as he'd lived most of that marriage — loving her in the quiet way a man does when he's convinced that protecting someone means keeping them at a distance.

As the hours blurred past midnight, Nardone shuffled through his scattered notes, crossing some out, circling others, crumpling up the ones that didn't belong. In his mind's eye, the puzzle was starting to take form — money, Russians, fear. But there were still gaps that gnawed at him.

Why, if they had money, were Mikael and Ilya living in a shabby one-bedroom flat in Old Slovenia?

Why were they so afraid, not just of the police, but of something bigger? And who were the three men in the Pontiac, barreling toward their building as if drawn by a magnet?

A memory flashed — the way Ilya's hands had trembled; the quick glance she'd shot Mikael before he snapped at her. Fear, yes. But not of the police. Fear of something closing in, something worse.

Chapter Four

Peter's Plan

It was late when Peter showed up at Taranov's flat with a
bottle of Armenian brandy and a stack of crumpled notes.
The others were out—Mikael working at the café, Ilya at
the library. Peter had insisted on coming alone.

Taranov answered the door in his undershirt, cigarette
already lit, eyes tired.

Peter grinned, lifted the bottle. "Fuel for revolutionary
minds."

Taranov let him in without a word.

They sat at the small kitchen table. The brandy went into
mismatched glasses, no toast.

Peter spread the papers across the table — diagrams, dates,
a rough sketch of a military plane.

Taranov didn't look at them.

Instead, he watched Peter.

"You've never liked details," he said finally. "When you
were a boy, you could barely finish a chess game. Too
impatient."

Peter shrugged. "Different kind of war now."

"Still requires patience."

Peter sipped and leaned back. "You're not sold on the plan."

"It's not the plan I'm unsure of," Taranov said. "It's the young man writing it."

Peter's grin faltered.

Taranov reached for the cigarette in the ashtray, tapped ash onto the floor. "You say this is about waking people up. About striking the system where it bleeds."

Peter nodded. "Because it is."

"But the money... the timing... the target," Taranov continued, "it all smells more like revenge than revolution."

Peter's expression hardened. "You think I'm doing this for my father?"

"I think," Taranov said slowly, "you're doing this because your father built a world that refused to see you. And now you want to burn it down with his name still on the mailbox."

Silence stretched.

Outside, distant sirens echoed across the river.

Peter didn't answer right away. He stared into his glass, swirling the amber liquid like it could offer some other truth.

"I was born into a system I didn't choose," he said at last. "I watched him lie to everyone — to colleagues, to party leaders, to my mother. And the worst part? He believed it was noble. That hoarding power, rationing hope — it was patriotic.”

Taranov’s voice softened. “So, this is personal.”

Peter looked up; expression tightened. “It was always personal. But that doesn’t make it wrong.”

“No,” Taranov said. “It just makes it dangerous.”

Peter stood suddenly, folding the pages with sharp, agitated hands. “You’ve lived in this rot longer than any of us. If anyone should want to take it down—”

“I’ve buried men for less,” Taranov said calmly. “And I’ve watched better men break because they couldn’t tell the difference between justice and vengeance.”

Peter stilled.

Then nodded.

“Maybe I don’t know the difference,” he admitted. “Maybe I don’t care anymore.”

Taranov sighed, then finished his drink in a single motion. He stood, went to the window, cracked it open to let the smoke escape.

“You’re a brilliant fool,” he said. “But I’ll help you. Not for the politics. Not for the money.”

He turned, eyes hard now. “I help because you’re still the boy I swore I’d protect. But don’t ask me to lie to myself about what this is.”

Peter gave a single, slow nod.

"Fair enough," he said quietly.

And then: "You're still in?"

Taranov took a final drag from the cigarette and crushed it against the sill.

"I'm in," he said. "But I won't save you from yourself, Petya. Not this time."

Peter didn't respond. He just poured them both another drink.

Outside, the night pressed against the glass like a held breath.

Taranov then listened to the plan as he always did, offering advice and questioning any possible short-comings, never thinking much would come from it. Peter asked Taranov if he knew of any older, retired Soviet pilots? And of course he did.

Two names were given and Peter reached out to a pair of disillusioned ex-military pilots, discarded by the system, bitter and itching for purpose. It wasn't hard to win them over.

As Taranov sat and listened to Peter's plan, he thought that this time might be a little more than just the vodka talking.

Ilya sat in the dim bar, watched the pilots across the table. Grigor, the elder, had deep lines around his mouth and a voice like gravel. "You want to rob the dragon," he said, raising a glass. "Be ready for the fire." Mikael's fingers tapped nervously on the table, but Peter only smiled, clinking his glass with Grigor's. "We're already burned," Peter said softly. "Might as well aim to fly higher."

Their small circle grew from three, to four with Taranov, then six, as they added the two pilots. Peter confided in them, explaining everything: the plan, the money, the stakes.

For Taranov, it was a once-in-a-lifetime opportunity — an escape from a system that promised him a hundred years of loyalty and delivered only cold duty.

For Peter, it was all about the message. For Ilya, it was about the future — she and Peter planned to marry once they escaped. For Mikael, it was less clear. He was the shadow in the room, the one who quietly wondered if they were all mad, even as he helped draw up maps and timetables.

Sometimes, late at night, Mikael would glance at Ilya across the table, watching the way her eyes lit when Peter spoke.

He'd wonder, just for a moment, what might have been — if the world were quieter, if Peter weren't a storm she couldn't resist. But he never said a word.

In Ilya's eyes, Peter was unlike anyone she had ever known. Where the black-market men in her family craved money for its own sake, Peter saw wealth as a tool, not an end. He loved art, culture, ideas. He respected money, but it didn't define him. It was that rare balance — ambition without greed — that fascinated her.

The Black Market was the largest criminal enterprise in the Soviet Union, but no one, not even the boldest thieves, dared strike at the Politburo itself. The thought alone was suicide.

And yet, that was what drew Peter. Because no one expected it.

In the late 80s the Soviets were already beginning to withdraw from Afghanistan, realizing it was a war that cost more than anything they could hope to gain. There were ethnic uprisings and protests all over the Soviet Union, and the KGB's central control was crumbling as tensions grew in the satellite countries that made up the Soviet Union.

In the dim glow of their apartment, huddled over worn maps and dog-eared schedules, the plan took shape.

Here's what they planned: They would hit the flight, hijack a Soviet Military transport plane before it took off toward Moscow, take as much of the American Dollars as they could, and vanish — leaving behind just enough money to suggest a mishap, to delay suspicion, to buy time.

The team's pilots would take off, get far enough away from Gorelevo and Leningrad, set the plane to explode, and bail out. They would float down to safety, disappear into the scenery outside of Leningrad, use the little bit of money they would stash, and work their way down to Athens and the rendezvous point.

"We'll leave fingerprints," Peter said one night, eyes glinting. "But the wrong kind." Ilya laughed softly, brushing a hand through his hair.

"We're either brilliant," she murmured, "or idiots." Mikael looked up from his notes, a rare smile gleaming across his face. "Why not both?"

It was, they told themselves, foolproof.

Of course, no plan survives its collision with reality.

And when that collision came, it wouldn't just scatter maps. It would burn lives, erase names, and leave only questions in its wake.

Chapter Five

Millions

By morning, Nardone's apartment smelled like cold coffee and takeout, and his alarm clock blinked insistently. Nardone barely noticed. Sleep would come later. Right now, adrenaline — better than caffeine — kept him upright.

In the precinct, Eva was already at her desk, sleeves rolled up, hair pulled back, focused. She'd slept like a rock — she always did.

Years ago, when she was studying psychology, she'd learned techniques for calming her mind. Back then, her professor had told the class to come up with a mantra for deep relaxation. She'd chosen one as a joke — "Relax, relax, relax" — but it stuck. These days, Eva could fall asleep the moment her head hit the pillow, a skill that served her well on this job.

She glanced up at the clock, frowned, then leaned back in her chair with a yawn. The bullpen around her buzzed — phones ringing, keyboards clattering, voices low and tense. She sipped coffee, watching the door, waiting.

When she saw Nardone walk in, eyes bloodshot, jaw set, she knew immediately: he hadn't slept at all. And that meant he was onto something.

"So," she asked, a spark of amusement in her voice, "what did you find?"

Nardone didn't answer right away. Instead, he dropped into his chair, stretched, and said, "Wrap up what you need to this morning. We're going for coffee."

Eva raised an eyebrow. She knew what that meant — not just coffee. This coffee meant off-site, out of earshot, where they could speak freely. And that meant something big.

She nodded, keeping her cool, but the word money echoed in the back of her mind. She dove into the morning's reports, but her pulse was already quickening.

She texted her brother while flipping through files — Can't talk. Big day. Will call tonight.

Her brother was all she had left in her life, both parents had passed away many years ago. This was somewhat monumental. She spoke to him nearly every morning.

But today, she could already feel the electricity in the air, the thrill that came when a case cracked open just enough to let the light in.

Time blurred. When Nardone finally appeared at her desk, jacket in hand, she was surprised how fast the hours had passed.

"You ready yet?" he asked quietly.

She grabbed her coat without a word.

As they stepped into the cool morning air, Eva felt it deep
in her bones: something was shifting. The pieces were
moving on the board, and whatever Nardone had
discovered overnight, it was going to change everything.

As they crossed the street, Eva fell into step beside him.
"You're not going to tell me anything until we sit down, are
you?"
Nardone gave her a sideways glance, lips twitching. "You
know me."
She sighed, smiling despite herself. "Yeah, unfortunately, I
do."

Nardone had sat at his desk late into the night before,
staring at his notes. He'd calculated the dimensions of the
boxes he'd seen, estimated the square footage of the
apartment, and run the numbers over and over.

By his best guess, there could be between sixty and eighty
million dollars stashed away in that tiny upstairs flat on the
Lower East Side.

"Fuck," he kept whispering to himself, the words looping
in his mind like a stuck cord.

Morning came and he pushed back from the desk, rubbing
a hand over his face, the stubble rasping against his palm.
His eyes burned from too much coffee and too little sleep.

Outside, the city murmured its restless lullaby — sirens,
distant car horns, the occasional bark of a stray dog. It was
the sound of lives grinding on, oblivious to the fortune
hidden in plain sight.

On the drive over with Sayers, neither of them said much.

They parked near the old neighborhood market and slipped into a corner booth at a run-down café.

The morning rush buzzed around them — clinking coffee mugs, murmured conversations — but inside their bubble, the world felt eerily still.

Sayers stirred her coffee absently, eyes glancing out of the window, watching an old man shuffle past with a cane, a paper bag swinging from one thin wrist.

She exhaled, long and slow. "You look like hell, John." "Thanks," Nardone muttered, cracking a faint smile. "Feel like it, too."

"Well," Sayers said finally, folding her hands on the table, "let me have it."

Nardone laid it out — everything he knew, everything he'd pieced together, everything he suspected. He told her about the money, the history, the probable connection to the explosion.

And when he was finished, Sayers leaned back against the booth, wide-eyed.

"Fuck," she murmured — the same word Nardone had muttered all night.

They sat in stunned silence.

For a moment, the sounds of the café faded — the clatter of dishes, the hiss of the espresso machine, the low murmur of conversation — until it was just the two of them, suspended between disbelief and possibility.

Sayers drummed her fingers on the table, eyes unfocused.

"That's a lot of money to be sitting in some apartment on the east side," Sayers finally said, her voice light, but with an edge of curiosity. She grinned. "Why isn't it in a bank account?

And… no one would miss ten or twenty million, right?"

Nardone cracked a tired grin. Truth was, the same thought had crossed his mind more than once.

He was a seasoned detective, a man of principles — or so he'd always told himself. But ten or twenty million dollars… that could change everything.

And if they didn't take it, if they left it sitting there, how long before someone else came along to claim it?

"It's like a live grenade," Nardone said softly, "just sitting there, waiting for someone to pull the pin."

Sayers tilted her head, considering. "So… what's keeping us from pulling it first?"

"That car explosion," he said, thinking aloud, "it has to have something to do with the money. And I'd bet they're not the first ones over the years who may have come looking."

That would explain why Mikael and Ilya lived so low-profile, why they clung to a modest life in a crumbling neighborhood when they were sitting on a literal fortune. They weren't hiding the money from the government — they were hiding it from everyone.

Sayers gave him a sly smile. "What would you do with half of twenty million?"

It was barely a joke — just the tiniest push.

Without missing a beat, Nardone answered, "I'd learn Italian, disappear into northern Italy, and never be seen again."

Sayers barked a laugh, shaking her head. "You? Retire to a vineyard? You'd last a month before you were asking the local police about any open cases."
"Maybe," Nardone admitted with a shrug, "but it'd be one hell of a month."

Sayers tilted her head, eyes glinting. "So… how are we going to do that?"

The moment hung in the air. The playful words weren't so playful anymore. And just like that, the line between fantasy and reality began to blur.

For a long moment, neither of them spoke. Sayers traced the rim of her coffee cup with one finger; lips parted like she wanted to speak but wasn't sure how to start.

Nardone watched the steam curl upward and wondered when exactly the shift had happened — when the thought stopped being ridiculous and started tasting like possibility.

Nardone was in his mid-forties, with over a decade on the force. Once, he'd been the golden boy — sharp, handsome, no-nonsense.

But the years had weathered him, carved lines into his face, dulled the edges of his confidence. Lately, the cracks showed.

He could feel it himself, in moments of restless exhaustion, in the way his colleagues glanced at him and quickly looked away.

He still remembered the call that broke something inside him.

Her name was Tessa Morales — twenty-three, terrified, and stupidly brave. She'd come forward to testify against her boyfriend, a mid-level heroin distributor with ties to a cartel. The department had promised her protection. The DA assured them she'd be safe.

Nardone had sat across from her in the interview room, watched her tremble as she described the violence, the deals, the late-night runs across county lines. He'd put a hand on hers, just briefly. "You're doing the right thing," he'd told her. "We've got you."

Two weeks later, her body was found behind a laundromat.

No forced entry. No sign of a struggle. Just silence and a single bullet behind the ear.

The DA blamed a paperwork error. The department blamed miscommunication. No one blamed themselves. But Nardone did.

He carried her picture in the back of an old notebook now — not out of guilt, but as a reminder. A reminder that good people died while the machine kept turning.

And now, maybe — just maybe — someone like him deserved a little something back for staying in it this long.

He used to dream about making captain, about leaving a legacy. Lately, though, the dream felt thin — stretched over too many years, too many compromises.

With this secret curled between his hands, the old ambitions felt almost laughable.

Sayers knew him better than anyone. She'd watched him struggle through the ups and downs — especially after his marriage fell apart.

He'd been blindsided, crushed by the betrayal, and for a long time, he'd tried to fix what was already gone.

It had taken him nearly two years to admit defeat, to let go. And even then, the pain hadn't really left. He carried it like a weight inside his chest, the kind that tightened late at night when the world went quiet.

Work was his anchor. When everything else crumbled, he poured himself into the job.

Sayers admired that — even as she worried what it was doing to him.

For her part, Sayers had never been one to settle down.

In her late thirties, sharp, witty, fiercely independent, she had made peace with the fact that her career came first.

Relationships faded; but work remained. Over the years, a deep respect had grown between her and Nardone, a friendship that, at times, edged toward something more — though neither of them dared cross that line.

They both shared this walk in life, and both knew the other had a storied life before coming back to this. Each had their buried secrets, their other lives, their other careers, but neither pried, just enjoying the company and working together now.

In moments like this — with possibility humming between them, with the rules bending ever so slightly — Sayers wondered if maybe, just maybe, they'd been waiting for the same thing all along. A reason to jump.

But now, seeing the old spark in his eyes, the fire she'd thought was long extinguished, Sayers felt the stirrings of something else she hadn't expected: excitement. Not just about the case, but about the man sitting across from her.

Back in his apartment, later that day, Nardone wrestled with the same thought on a loop: Could I really walk away from everything I've built?

Ten million dollars. That was the number his brain kept circling back to. People liked to say money couldn't buy happiness. Maybe not. But it sure as hell could buy a way out of misery.

He stood at the window, watching the city lights blink against the dark, and tried to picture his life in another place — somewhere the past couldn't follow, where the badge didn't define him.

For the first time in years, the thought didn't feel like failure. It felt like possibility.

He was a decorated detective, just a few years from retirement. On paper, his life looked respectable, even enviable.

But in the quiet of his own mind, he knew: the temptation wasn't a question of if, it was now a question of how.

He just needed to know Sayers was on board.

And judging by her half-smile at the café, by the glint of mischief in her eyes, that wouldn't take much convincing.

The game had already begun.

Outside, a police siren wailed past, fading into the distance. Nardone exhaled, a slow, measured breath. Tomorrow would bring questions, decisions, risks. But tonight — just for tonight — the world was wide open.

Chapter Six

The Heist

The weeks of planning, acquiring counterfeit travel documents, waiting, and nervous rehearsals had all come down to this night.

Peter and Mikael had poured over schedules for weeks — planes, deliveries, guard rotations, weather forecasts. Tonight was the night they had chosen: the first night of the rest of their new lives.

Ilya had barely touched her dinner, her fingers trembling as she lit one cigarette after another, pacing the apartment in tight circles.

Mikael sat quietly by the window, watching the city fade into dusk, fingers tapping a nervous rhythm on the windowsill.

Peter, by contrast, moved with the grace of a man who had convinced himself everything was inevitable — he poured a shot of vodka, offered it to Mikael, and grinned. "To history," he murmured. Mikael clinked his glass without a word.

They made their way to the airfield, slipping into the back of a small military truck driven by their two pilot accomplices.

A couple bottles of decent vodka was all it took to keep the gate guards distracted — just another uneventful Leningrad night, or so they thought.

The team was in position now, waiting near the runway as the night air bit cold against their skin.

Ilya pulled her coat tighter, shivering. "Remind me why we're not in Mexico right now," she muttered.
Peter smiled. "Because Mexico doesn't change the world."

Mikael exhaled through his nose, watching the plumes curl in the freezing air. "Neither does dying in a Siberian prison."

Their spotter signaled: the truck was nearly empty. The shipment — the one they'd been tracking for weeks — was loaded onto the waiting transport plane.

All that remained was for the flight crew to be notified, and the rest would unfold like clockwork.

They hadn't known the exact size of the shipment, but the whispers were clear: this was one of the biggest hauls of the year.

On the plane, there was only a three-man loading crew. Normally, the total detail should have been nine, but tonight the airfield was asleep. Half the men were drinking and gambling in the breakroom, and the unlucky three out here on the tarmac had drawn the short straws.

The truck rolled into position.

They moved as they'd practiced a dozen times — onto the truck, onto the plane, neutralizing the loaders without firing a shot.

To call it a fight was generous; the men were too drunk, too exhausted to do more than blink in surprise before they were tied up and stashed in the back of the plane.

One loader let out a faint groan as they bound his hands. Ilya crouched beside him, pressing a finger to her lips. "Shh," she whispered, voice soft as a lullaby. His eyes fluttered closed, and she stood, heart pounding so hard she thought it might crack her ribs.

They transferred all but a few decoy crates back onto the truck, leaving just enough aboard to maintain the illusion that everything was proceeding as scheduled. Then they waited, nerves tight as guitar strings.

Peter kept checking his watch, lips moving silently as he counted down the minutes.

Mikael watched the pilots through the cockpit window, fingers twitching.

Ilya leaned against the cold metal of the plane, eyes closed, whispering a prayer she wasn't sure she believed anymore.

When the official flight crew arrived, Peter's team was ready.

The pilots barely had time to register confusion before they were overpowered and bound, joining the loaders in the hold.

Peter's pilot and co-pilot slipped into the cockpit, running through the preflight checks as smoothly as if they'd never been gone.

Meanwhile, the truck rumbled off the tarmac, Peter, Ilya, Mikael, and Taranov aboard. So far, it was going even better than they had hoped.

They navigated toward the city, the night thick with the scent of victory.

In the backseat, Ilya let out a shaky laugh, burying her face in Peter's shoulder. "We're actually doing this," she murmured. Peter kissed the top of her head, his own grin wide and reckless.

Mikael, riding shotgun, kept glancing in the mirror, unease etched deep into his features. "Don't celebrate yet," he muttered. "It's not over."

In the tower, the first tremors of suspicion were beginning to crack the calm.

The controller began requesting the clearance codes. Silence. Again, the request crackled over the radio. Still nothing.

At first, the controller tried to reassure himself: A glitch, surely. A radio malfunction. But protocol was clear — when in doubt, stop the flight. He radioed a maintenance crew to intercept the plane on the taxiway and immediately roused the base's military security.

The security team scrambled from their drunken haze. Nothing sobered a man faster than an emergency call.

Within moments, two trucks were racing across the dark tarmac toward the transport.

Inside the cockpit, the senior pilot, Grigor, cursed under his breath, hands flying over the controls.

"They're onto us," he barked. The co-pilot's jaw clenched as he flipped switches, sweat beading on his forehead. "We've got maybe sixty seconds before they block the runway."

In the cockpit, the pilots saw the headlights approaching. The lead pilot cursed under his breath, shoved the throttles forward, and began the lumbering roll toward the runway.

Outside, the security drivers were yelling into their radios, their passengers fumbling with rifles.

"Soprovazhdaite yego! Soprovazhday!" — Force them to stop! the controller shouted, his voice cracking with panic.

As the plane began its turn onto the main runway, the security trucks closed in. But no one wanted to get too close. Those roaring propellers were as lethal as any weapon.

The aircraft's engines howled, the nose lifting slightly. Inside the trucks, the soldiers yelled over each other: "Strelyai! Strelyai!" — Shoot! Shoot! Gunfire rattled into the night, rounds pinging harmlessly off the old transport's reinforced hull.

Ilya, watching from the truck as they sped down the access road, gripped Peter's arm. "They're shooting," she breathed, panic threading her voice.

Peter's hand found hers, squeezed hard. "They won't stop it in time," he whispered, as much to himself as to her.

As they drove, Ilya's eyes glazed over, not just from fear, but memory. She saw her uncle again, standing in a queue that wrapped around a cracked stone building, cradling his shoes against his chest like a child. He'd waited six hours that day.

They gave him a ration ticket for socks. "It's not about the shoes," he had whispered to her once. "It's about being reminded you have no control over anything."

Peter stared out the opposite window, jaw clenched. In his mind's eye, his father stood at the balcony of their childhood apartment — cigarette in one hand, oblivion in the other. "Some people are born to lead, Petya. The rest follow. Best you understand that now."

That night, Peter had quietly taken a chessboard from his uncle Dmitri's bag and hidden it in his room, as if defiance could be held in check by thirty-two carved pieces.

Mikael reached into his coat pocket and traced the edge of his leather-bound notebook. In his head, a line from Mandelstam came unbidden: We live without feeling the country beneath us. He didn't know why it surfaced, only that it felt like truth.

In the tower, the controller's voice hit a fever pitch. "Stolknutsya s nim! Run into him! Stolknutsya!"

One of the trucks veered hard, the driver gritting his teeth, trying to swing in behind the tail. But the plane was already surging forward, engines screaming, the nose lifting off the runway. They were seconds too late.

And then the nightmare escalated.

What Peter hadn't known — what none of them had known — was that this airbase had a standing Air Defense Forces/ADF unit. Soviet history had made sure of that.

"Vzlyot!" — Scramble! came the order. Two MiG-23 fighters roared down a parallel runway, engines glowing like molten steel, the ground trembling under their wheels.

In the car, Mikael slammed a fist against the dashboard. "Bozhe Moy," he rasped, eyes wide as he watched the fighter jets take off.

Ilya buried her face in her hands, muffling a sob. Peter clenched his jaw so hard it ached, fingers digging into his knees as if sheer willpower could bend the outcome their way.

The air traffic controller, white-faced and sweating, had already attempted to have the Base Commander awakened.

The night orderly, assigned to awaken the Commander knew this would be like awakening a bear from hibernation, and he ignored it and then delayed it as long as possible.

Once the dread passed, and he grew more afraid of "NOT" having awoken the Commander – he jumped to his task.

And within moments, the commander was patched through to the ADF ground controller.

"Target is a passenger transport aircraft, TU-154. Report when you have visual."

Seconds passed.

"Tsel vizhu." — I see the target.

"Pusk razreshon." — Permitted to engage.

Two air-to-air rockets streaked into the night.

On the ground, Peter's team watched in horror, frozen as the first blast of flame lit the horizon. The sky cracked open, a second sun igniting above the frozen fields.

Ilya didn't scream. She couldn't. The sound caught in her throat and turned to static. She clawed at the seatbelt, ripping it loose, lunged from the car into the snow.

She fell to her knees, vomiting. Not from what she had seen — from the grief, the guilt, the explosion of everything she believed about right and wrong.

Mikael knelt beside Ilya and said nothing. Just placed his hand on her back. And for the first time since they began, he felt the weight of their sins, heavy as ash in the cold air.

Peter closed his eyes, His hands rested on his knees, fingers
white from the pressure. His lips formed the numbers —
minutes, seconds — the countdown they'd practiced.

He didn't speak then. He just sat, lips moving, eyes hollow
hoping the pilots made it out safely — and for the first time
in his life, felt the full, brutal weight of what it meant to
gamble everything.

Chapter Seven

So, what's the move?

Nardone and Sayers traded ideas across the table, sketching out a rough plan on a napkin: take the money, stage an explosion, leave just enough behind to fool whoever came looking. A gas leak, maybe. An electrical fire. Something believable, something final.

Sayers tapped the pen against her lip, brow furrowed. "You really think a fire buys us enough time?"

"It buys us a head start," Nardone murmured.
"And after the head start?"

He gave her a long look. "Then we stop running."
For the first time that morning, Sayers' grin faltered.

And yet, beneath their words, an unspoken tension hummed.

Neither wanted to say it out loud, but both knew: this wasn't just about stealing money. This was about survival.

That night, after a frustrating day of cold leads and bureaucratic dead-ends, Nardone lay in bed staring at the ceiling, his mind racing.

The ceiling fan hummed softly overhead, blades slicing the dark. His apartment smelled faintly of old coffee and rain — the window left cracked open to the night.

He exhaled, slow and shaky, willing his body to relax. It didn't work. His muscles hummed with tension, nerves stretched thin, his chest tight with the sense that the clock was running out.

Sleep hovered just out of reach.

And then — like a flashbulb in the dark — it hit him.

He sat bolt upright, heart hammering, the pieces clicking together in an instant.

The crash. The weapons. The Russian couple.

The three dead men hadn't been aimless criminals. They were soldiers on a mission, headed somewhere with purpose, armed to the teeth. They knew where the money was.

And if they knew, others did too.

If those men didn't return, someone else would come — and soon.

This isn't about theft anymore, Nardone realized. This is about who's left standing.

A cold rush shot through him, like plunging into ice water. He ran a hand through his hair, the sharp sting of realization cutting through the fog of exhaustion.

This wasn't just a score. It was a fuse burning fast.

He grabbed his phone and typed a single message.

Nardone: Coffee. Now.

Sayers was already pulling on her jacket when the text arrived. She didn't need details; she just needed the destination.

They met at an all-night diner — their sanctuary, their war room. It was the kind of place where the regulars came to disappear into greasy plates of food and bottomless coffee cups, where the staff knew better than to ask questions, and where no one gave a damn who was whispering in the corner booth at 2 a.m.

When she arrived, Nardone was there, as always, with his back to the wall, his eyes on the door and the side entrance to the kitchen.

Their booth was shadowed, a single bulb shining down from overhead. He'd already ordered two coffees.

One sat untouched across from him, steam curling in the dim light. His fingers drummed restlessly on the tabletop, a quiet tattoo of nerves.

She slid into the booth across from him, her hair still damp from the shower, her face bare of the usual workday polish.

"You're getting predictable, you know that?" she teased softly. But the edge in her voice was tight with worry.

Nardone gave the faintest hint of a smile, then leaned in, his voice low.

"We're out of time."

Sayers swallowed hard. "How many others know?"

"Enough," Nardone murmured, eyes locked on hers.

"Enough to make this a race. And if we wait even one more day, we're not walking away with anything."

Her fingers tightened around the coffee mug. For a moment, she looked down, jaw clenched, as if weighing some silent equation. Then she looked up, meeting his gaze squarely. "We were never really just talking about the money, were we?"

"They knew where they were going…" Nardone said softly as Sayers sat back into the booth across from him.

She gave him a slightly puzzled look, head tilting just a fraction. He could tell immediately — she had no idea what he was talking about.

The café was half-empty, the late-night crowd thinning, the air thick with the smell of stale coffee and faint traces of disinfectant.

Outside, the streetlights buzzed, throwing pale halos onto the wet pavement. Nardone's eyes were sharp, feverish almost, the adrenaline of his realization still surging through him.

"The three guys in the explosion — the car, the weapons…" he began, leaning forward, his voice low and urgent.

"Right, right, right…" Sayers murmured, nodding just enough to keep him talking. In truth, she was still trying to catch up.

But she knew from experience — if she stayed quiet, if she kept giving him small murmurs of agreement, he'd lay it all out.

And he did.

"One of the three has already been identified as ex-Russian Spetsnaz," Nardone said, his fingers drumming lightly on the tabletop. "They were on their way to the apartment.

They knew exactly where they were going. They knew what they were going to find. They knew where the money was."

The words came like bullets, fast and sharp.

Sayers felt the edge of her pulse quicken, the way it always did when a case snapped into sharp focus — when the pieces, scattered and stubborn for days, finally began to lock together.

She leaned forward slightly, brow furrowing, the noise of the café fading into the background hum of her thoughts.

"I'm sure that over the years, since it disappeared, the legend of where the money ended up has grown. And just guessing from what we saw in that flat —" he let out a dry laugh, shaking his head — "I don't think the legends have even caught up to the real amount."

Sayers sat back slowly; her arms crossed.

A cold, sinking feeling pooled in her gut. This wasn't the sort of thing you contained with a few patrol cars and some yellow tape. This was the kind of thing that chewed through neighborhoods, through cities, through anyone dumb enough to get in its way.

Now it was starting to come together in her mind.

Forget the cash, forget the fantasy of ten or twenty million tucked under a mattress — this was a powder keg. This wasn't just a heist waiting to happen; it was a war waiting to break out.

Her chest tightened slightly as the realization hit.

The quiet families, the corner shop owners, the old men feeding pigeons in Old Slovenia — none of them had the faintest idea what was sitting in their midst.

And when the wolves came, they wouldn't care who got trampled on the way to the kill.

Regardless of the money, regardless of the fortune gathering dust in that flat, people were going to come looking. And when they came, they wouldn't knock.

They would tear through Old Slovenia like a storm.

For all her cynicism, for all the years she'd worked in a system that seemed to care more about paperwork than people, Sayers still believed in something simple at her core — the job was about serving and protecting.

And if what Nardone was describing was true, they were sitting on a live grenade in the middle of their city.

Someone would come again. It was just a matter of time.

She looked at Nardone, her voice quieter now. "So, what's the move?"

He exhaled, tapping his thumb against the edge of his coffee cup. "We bring Mikael and Ilya in for questioning.

We clear the building, make sure everyone's out.

We move the boxes, we blow the apartment, and we leave just enough money behind to throw off the trail."

Sayers let out a soft whistle, running a hand through her hair. "Jesus, John… you've been busy."

"Didn't have much choice," he murmured. "The clock's ticking."

Chapter Eight

Collapse

Within moments, fire crews from Gorelovo were racing toward the smoldering wreckage of the TU-154.

By the time they arrived, flames were already burning down, their job less about saving the plane and more about securing the scene.

Men in heavy coats shouted orders over the crackle of radios, their breath fogging in the cold dawn air. The blackened carcass of the plane hissed and steamed; metal twisted into grotesque shapes.

One firefighter, young and wide-eyed, stared too long before his commander cuffed the back of his helmet.

"Move," the man barked. "This isn't a circus."

Thankfully, the night's active runway had carried the transport away from the city before it went down. But that was little comfort.

By sunrise, the entire base was on lockdown, and within hours, one of the largest military investigations in recent Soviet history would begin.

The Soviets locked down the entire city around Gorelovo, going from door to door looking for anyone who might have had some information on the crash of a military aircraft, not giving any clues as to the importance.

There were no survivors of the shoot down, and there were no traces of anyone who might have been involved in the hijacking.

Nothing like this had ever happened. There had been instances of Soviet pilots drunk and taking an aircraft out, but for the most part, they came back, were disciplined and life moved on.

The first reports to higher ups were that a plane had been hijacked by perpetrators who had knowledge of Soviet Military flight protocol, alluding to former Soviet Pilots, and that it had been a routine transport.

It had only been a few days since the incident, and the story leaked on 8 March, 1988 to the Leningrad Vedomosti and what went out to the public and the rest of the world was that a passenger airliner, Aeroflot Flight 3379 had been highjacked by a group of armed criminals and that they had been killed or captured.

Peter's father knew more of the story. He knew that it wasn't a standard military supply flight, it had been carrying a large sum of currency. In the classified report version he had eyes on, tatters of burned American Dollars and other currencies had been falling for miles around the Gorelovo and the Annino area outside of Leningrad.

No one initially had an idea of what had actually transpired, that three university students had masterminded the biggest cash heist in Soviet history, and were currently sitting on millions of dollars in a Greek city a thousand miles away.

After the first week Peter's father knew something was wrong. He would go days without hearing from Peter, but he would be home on weekends for clean clothes and to rest and study for the next week of classes or wanting funds replenished in the summer, but not this time.

He began to have nagging parental thoughts, wondering if his son could have been hurt, or somehow involved, telling himself that his absurd thoughts were just that – nonsense.

Moscow — Department V (Financial Intelligence)
December 2, 1989

The room was underground — a vault beneath a vault, three floors below the Ministry of Foreign Economic Relations. The air was always dry. Cold. Everything inside was steel and silence.

Comrade Vasily Orlov turned the page slowly, his gloved finger tracing each entry line by line.

The serial numbers were handwritten at first — copied from melted scraps of U.S. currency recovered near the Gorelovo wreckage. Much of it was ash, but some survived. Hardened by fire. Stiff with grease. Pieces of a much larger puzzle.

He compared them to the Registry of Controlled Foreign Currency Assets, an unofficial logbook maintained off-record — even from many inside the KGB.

What he found chilled him more than the room.

"Serials 3319 through 3340… recorded as part of Red Flag Shipment 17, routed for political stabilization funds in East Africa. Sealed in Vault C. Reported unmoved."

Vasily leaned back, heart thudding.

The serials hadn't just gone missing.

They had never been released.

Which meant the crash at Gorelovo hadn't been an accident.

It had been a heist.

Later that afternoon, upstairs the Deputy Director for Department V, a man with a voice like granite and hands that never shook, tapped a red pencil against a printed memo.

"They burned the plane to hide the theft," he said flatly. "But fire doesn't burn serial numbers."

Vasily stood quietly across the desk.

"You're certain?" the Director asked.

Vasily nodded once. "We matched over two dozen bills already. Same series. Vault-sealed. Never intended for circulation."

The Director exhaled slowly through his nose.

"Who knows?"

"No one outside this room. The Central Bank's own audit logs list the funds as untouched."

The Director gave a slow, grim smile. "Good. Then we'll be the ones to find it."

He stood, stepped to a map pinned across the far wall. Lines marked recent reports — Athens, Naples, Belgrade.

"We will not report to the Politburo yet. We will not issue an Interpol request, not until we are sure."

He circled Athens in red.

"Start watching flagged serials through Mediterranean exchanges. Use shell intermediaries — banks, casinos, black market vendors. Any currency that hits a scanner gets uploaded and matched."

"And if we find a match?"

The Director looked out the frost-rimmed window.

"Then we send someone."

Four days later in a cramped office above an exchange booth in Monastiraki, a wire flickered to life.

A banknote validation system at a port-side casino in Piraeus had flagged two U.S. bills — $100 notes, clean and crisp — with serials that fell inside the suspected stolen range.

The technician didn't know the significance. He just did his job and uploaded the flagged codes.

Three blocks away, a fax machine in a rented KGB-affiliate office sputtered to life.

A match.

In their rented apartment, Ilya and Mikael, Peter, and Taranov were just finishing lunch. Lentil soup. A crust of bread. Nothing remarkable.

Outside, the city of Athens buzzed always — traffic, horns, the clang of trolley bells. It was an ordinary day.

And somewhere across town, two plain men stepped into a car with a photograph in hand and a new directive:

"Confirm. Observe. Do not engage until instructed."

The noose had begun to tighten.

And they didn't even know it yet.

Peter, Mikael, Ilya, and Taranov, in Athens with its sunlit squares, cups of bitter Greek coffee, tried to pretend that they were ordinary travelers.

Athens in summer was a living paradox — cracked marble underfoot and golden light on crumbling walls, the scent of time rising from every corner.

The air was thick with the perfume of dust and orange blossoms, hot stone radiating upward long after sunset.

Heat clung to the skin like a second shirt, salty and dry, layered with exhaust and the ghost of olive oil from distant kitchens.

Somewhere down the hill, a butcher's shop opened early and closed before the sun could sear its wares, while fishmongers shouted in fast Greek that echoed like a chant through the alleys.

Even the pigeons here seemed ancient, cooing lazily from marble ledges that had outlived empires.

Plaster peeled from the sides of ochre-colored buildings, exposing older brick beneath — like skin revealing scars. The temples were always there, unmoved.

Whether glimpsed from the shade of a café awning or cresting a hill at dusk, the Acropolis stood like an accusation against time.

Mikael had never imagined a place could be both sanctuary and snare.

The city vibrated with life: motorbikes weaving through impossible traffic, laundry snapping in the breeze like flags of quiet resistance, bells from an Orthodox church tolling noon as if the hour itself was sacred.

Yet for every moment of wonder, there was a shadow that trailed them — in the reflection of sunglasses, the too-long pause of a passerby, the shrill ring of a payphone no one answered.

At night, the city cooled, but never quite breathed. The streets filled with murmured conversation and clinking glasses, and the smell of grilled lamb and anise lingered above sidewalk tables.

Athens was beautiful, yes — but never comfortable. It was history pressing in on all sides, whispering in broken columns and spray-painted slogans: *you are being watched by centuries.*

By day, the square was alive with voices and music, children darting between marble columns, the scent of roasted chestnuts drifting on the breeze.

Tourists snapped photos, lovers strolled arm in arm, and the ancient city hummed around them as if nothing in the world had changed.

At their table, a different current ran beneath the surface — the tremor of hunted animals, holding still only because they didn't know which way to bolt.

For days, they came back to the same spot in the square for lunch or a quiet coffee in the afternoons.

Surrounded by the breathtaking beauty of the white marble columns, the crumbling temples, and the electric hum of history all around them, it should have been paradise.

But none of them could let down their guard or relax.

Ilya wore sunglasses even at dusk, her fingers always fidgeting with a cigarette or the edge of a napkin.

Mikael rarely spoke, his eyes checking from face to face, memorizing strangers, logging exits.

Peter, always the optimist, forced a smile, telling jokes in low tones that earned only tight laughs.

And Taranov — Taranov watched everything, even his own people, like a man who trusted no one and nothing but gravity.

For the first week, they reassured themselves — maybe the two pilots were just slow making their way through customs, working their route south.

After all, the pilots didn't have the luxury of traveling with a KGB agent like Taranov, someone who could slip through borders with a smile, a firm handshake, or a quiet payoff.

By the second week, the optimism began to crack.

Chapter Nine

The FrostVault Job

Peter's father had to report on his son's absence and of his assigned man – Taranov. This set in motion more investigation, tapping his phones for any calls in or out.

Unbeknownst to him, was the number of bodies found in the wreckage, and the fact that none of them remotely resembled his son or Taranov.

Moscow, November 1989
Central State Bank – Sublevel Two

The lights hummed in the hallway — pale, flickering tubes that cast long shadows on the polished stone floor. It was nearly midnight. Snow dusted the windows six stories above, but the man in the hallway was sweating through his collar.

Vitaly Shvets had overseen internal finance audits for the State Bank for seventeen years. He had worked under Brezhnev, Andropov, Chernenko. He had watched the old guard die off in a parade of dull funerals and stiff eulogies. He had survived them all by saying little and knowing everything.

Tonight, he wished he knew less.

The thick folder in his hand bore the red band of classified material. The header read:
CASE: GORELOVO 11/12/89 — MILITARY TRANSPORT LOSS

ADDENDUM: CURRENCY SERIAL TRACE REQUEST

Inside: wreckage photos, melted wiring, aerial shots of scattered debris outside Leningrad.

And — worst of all — the itemized table.

Rows upon rows of U.S. Dollar serial numbers.

He ran a finger down the list, heart hammering. Some were charred. Some partially legible. But enough were clear to confirm the impossible.

These bills weren't supposed to exist outside the vaults.

Not in flight. Not unsupervised. Not at all.

The door ahead opened with a quiet click. A slim man in a black wool coat stepped into the hallway.

"Comrade Shvets," he said, nodding once. "Come."

The interior office smelled of old books and radiator dust. Behind the desk sat Deputy Chairman Kravchenko, face half-obscured in shadow. He gestured to the chair but didn't offer tea. That was how Shvets knew this wasn't just serious.

It was dangerous.

"Well?" Kravchenko asked.

Shvets opened the folder slowly. "The American currency aboard the downed flight— it was... not a standard transfer."

"How not standard?"

"These bills," Shvets said, tapping the serial list, "match allocations recorded as stored beneath Vault C. In Moscow. Two years ago."

Kravchenko went still. "Vault C has never been compromised."

Shvets didn't answer.

After a beat, Kravchenko leaned forward, voice dropping. "How much?"

Shvets hesitated. Then: "The total volume destroyed or stolen — preliminary estimate — exceeds 180 million U.S. dollars."

The silence that followed was thick with heat and history.

Shvets swallowed. "If this gets out, the image of financial control... of party unity... collapses."

Kravchenko pinched the bridge of his nose, muttering, "This is not a theft. This is a message."

He stood and turned toward the darkened window. "Do we know who orchestrated it?"

"No. But we do know it was internal. The flight manifest was fabricated. Access logs falsified. And only two people ever had direct sign-off on those vault pallets."

Kravchenko turned, eyes narrowing. "Who?"

Shvets didn't answer.

He didn't have to.

Kravchenko stepped slowly around the desk, voice soft now. "You're telling me someone with access to Politburo-level storage helped fund a theft that was covered with military clearance?"

He placed both hands on the back of Shvets' chair. "You're telling me someone with a family member in the Central Bank—"

"I'm telling you we don't know anything for certain," Shvets interrupted, his voice tight. "Only that the cover-up has already begun. And whoever pulled this off had help. Likely from one of our own."

Kravchenko's mouth twisted into something between a grimace and a smile.

"Then we must offer a reward," he said softly. "International."

"That risks exposure."

"So does losing track of 180 million dollars."

He walked to the shelf, picked up a crystal decanter, and poured a splash of brandy into a glass. He didn't offer Shvets any.

"When wolves take from your house," Kravchenko said, "you don't whisper about it. You set traps. You make the world smell blood."

He raised his glass.

"To loyalty," he murmured.

Shvets nodded slowly, the folder still open in his lap.

As he left the office fifteen minutes later, two thoughts chased him down the corridor like footsteps he couldn't see:

1. Whoever pulled this off was no longer in Russia.
2. Someone high up didn't want them found.

He would keep the second part to himself. For now.

Chapter Ten

Moral Compass

For years, Sayers prided herself on being the moral one —
the compass when others veered. But lately, the badge felt
less like a shield and more like a chain. And the idea of
walking away — of choosing herself for once — didn't
sound like betrayal. It sounded like breathing.

Eva Sayers used to believe in clean lines. Rules. Protocol.
Moral north stars.

As a child, she once turned in her own father — not for a
crime, but for lying. He'd told her mother he'd quit
smoking. Eva, ten years old and smug with righteousness,
had found the cigarettes in the garage.

At dinner, she'd waited for the right moment. Her mom
was talking about someone's promotion at work, her
brother picking the cheese off his lasagna. Then Eva said,
calm as a detective, "Daddy still smokes. He hides them
behind the paint cans."

The silence that followed had felt like judgment. But not on
him — on her.

Later that night, her mother pulled her aside. "We don't
turn on family," she'd said, her voice low but tight with
warning. "Even when we're right."

Eva never forgot that.
And yet, she kept doing it.

In high school, she reported a teacher for changing a grade. In college, she exposed a hazing ring in her dorm.

In her early days on the force, she logged a formal complaint against her training officer for pocketing cash during a raid.

None of it made her popular.
But she slept at night.

Until Michelle.

Michelle Torres had been Eva's first real case as lead investigator — a domestic violence situation no one wanted to touch.

The guy was ex-military, loud, careful, mean. Michelle had come in twice before with a bruised rib and a fake smile.

Everyone said the same thing: "She won't leave. It's a waste of time."

But Eva didn't see a waste. She saw someone afraid.

She took extra shifts. She stayed late to comb through Michelle's phone records, built a pattern of control and fear.

When Michelle finally agreed to testify, Eva helped her find a temporary shelter, bought her toiletries out of her own pocket, and promised her it would be okay.

"I won't let him near you," Eva had said. "Not ever again."

And she'd meant it.

Until a supervisor — tight with city brass, running for a council seat — decided the optics weren't great. No charges. Just a restraining order. Case closed.

Two weeks later, Michelle was found in her car, seatbelt still fastened, a cigarette in her hand, and her skull shattered from behind.

Eva sat through the funeral with her fists clenched under the pew. The guy walked. "No witnesses," the DA said. "Circumstantial."

Eva kept her job. But something cracked.

That night, she sat in her car outside her apartment for an hour, staring at the dashboard. At the time, she thought maybe she'd quit. Maybe she'd go into private security.

But in the end, she didn't. She kept showing up. Kept doing the work.

Just with a little less faith.

Now, years later, when Nardone asked her over stale diner coffee, "What would you do with ten million?" she didn't laugh like she should've. She didn't scoff, or roll her eyes, or rattle off a joke about a boat in Sicily.

She thought about Michelle.

She thought about every moment she'd followed the rules, and still someone wound up dead, alone, scared, or buried beneath a system designed to pretend it cared.

And she thought, maybe this time, the rules don't deserve to win.

That thought scared her more than she'd admit.

But it didn't leave.

For a long moment, they just sat there, the noise of the diner fading to a dull hum around them.

Finally, Sayers broke the silence. "You're sure about this?"

Nardone's jaw tightened, his gaze back and forth from the door, then back to her.

"I'm sure we either make our move now… or we watch someone else make it first — with a hell of a lot more blood. And not just some punk crew from Queens,"

Nardone added. "These are ex-military. Spetsnaz, maybe. These guys don't knock — they burn."

She let out a slow breath. "Then I guess we stop planning and start doing."

A tired laugh escaped Nardone, more breath than sound. "Didn't think it'd be you and me against the world," he murmured.

Sayers' lips curved into a small, fierce smile. "Yeah, well… the world doesn't stand a chance."

Outside, a siren wailed faintly in the distance. Inside, their booth became a small, tense island in a sea of clinking plates and muted conversation.

For the first time in days, Nardone felt clear. This wasn't about theory anymore.

This was the point where plans became action — and where good men found out what they were willing to become.

As they rose to leave, Nardone reached for his coat, pausing just long enough to meet her eyes. "You in?"

Sayers gave a soft snort. "John, I was in before you even asked."

They stepped out into the cold dawn, the wind whipping past them like it was trying to warn them back. But they didn't look back. Not once.

She commented quietly. "You always did love a good countdown."

There was a pause — a heavy, thoughtful silence.

"It's clean," Sayers murmured. "Simple."

"Yeah," Nardone said, his eyes gazing toward the window, watching the night beyond. "Beautiful, even — in theory."

But they both knew better.

A plan on paper was one thing. A plan in the dirt, under fire, with lives on the line — that was another beast entirely.

Sayers could already feel the variables piling up: panicked neighbors, unpredictable suspects, the wrong person in the wrong place at the wrong time. She took a slow breath, steadying herself.

Chapter Eleven

Have to leave - Now

Peter and Taranov had seen the plane lift off the runway. That should have been safety. But as they sat on park benches or in quiet cafés, voices low and eyes wary, they began to whisper the darker possibilities.

A million things could have gone wrong — interception, mechanical failure, betrayal, capture.

The silence from home was deafening.

Late at night, in their rented apartment, Peter would pace while Mikael stared at the ceiling.

Ilya, sleepless, lay curled on the couch, clutching an old sweater of Peter's like a lifeline. Taranov smoked by the window, the red glow of his cigarette the only light in the room.

"They should have called by now," Peter murmured one night, and Taranov gave a thin smile that didn't touch his eyes.

"They're not calling," he said softly. "You know that."

Taranov, hardened by years of espionage, was the only one who seemed to handle this stress.

With them, for the first time in years, Taranov let slip a bit of his true personality — a dry wit, a subtle charm, glimpses of a man buried beneath the spy.

He taught Ilya how to spot a tail in the crowd, teased Mikael into laughing for the first time in weeks, even shared half a bottle of ouzo with Peter one night on the rooftop.

"In another life," Taranov murmured, lifting his glass to the stars and pausing for effect, "we'd all be dead already."

Taranov ensured that very little of the money was touched, not wanting to attract any attention to a band of tourists with big spending habits. That small thing might have saved them in the beginning.

With his skill and background, he was still hesitant to reach back home.

Three weeks later, they knew they couldn't stay frozen in place forever. Someone had to test the waters.

They chose Taranov.

He found a payphone a mile from the square, well away from the guesthouse where they were hiding. Dropping a coin into the slot, he dialed Peter's father.

The voice that answered was strained, on the edge of panic.

Peter's father spoke in rapid Russian, his words trembling at the edges. "Peter? Is he there? Please tell me where you are—" Taranov cut in smoothly, voice all warmth and reassurance, slipping into his role like an old coat.

Taranov slipped easily into this, his tone light, a touch amused. "Everything's fine, sir," he confidently assured the older man. "Peter just needed to get away, clear his head before school begins again. You know how impulsive your son can be."

He danced carefully around the conversation, tossing out harmless pleasantries, watching for anything Peter's father might let slip. He probed gently, turning questions back on the older man, listening for clues.

But there was nothing. No hints, no murmured warnings. Just concern, confusion, and exhaustion, and he knew others had heard that message.

When Peter's father asked where they were, Taranov deflected smoothly — this was old training, muscle memory.

They both knew the lines were tapped. They both knew how this dance was done. What he didn't expect, as short as Taranov had made the call, was that the Soviets had an idea of where they were.

The technology to bug, wire, and intercept calls had advanced exponentially since he had been in the real mix of KGB activities.

When he returned to the apartment, the others were waiting, tense, hungry for any scrap of news.

He relayed the conversation in full, not omitting a single detail. And when he finished, they all sat in a heavy silence.

There was no signal in that call. Nothing to chase. No safe return, no new lead, no miracle.

They were, in every way, on their own.

Ilya's head dropped into her hands. Mikael leaned forward, elbows on his knees, face pale.

Peter let out a slow, shuddering breath, the weight of it pushing him deeper into the couch.

Taranov poured himself a drink, his fingers steady, his face unreadable. "We knew this," he said quietly. "We just didn't want to believe it."

The weeks stretched on, and with each passing day, the weight of reality pressed down harder.

Back in the sleepless nights of planning, soaked in vodka and defiance, they had mapped out every step of the heist.

But they had never thought past it — never asked what came next, what the rest of their lives would look like.

Now, they understood.

They could never go back.

They could never tell the truth.

And they would never truly stop running.

The money they'd taken had bought them freedom — but it came wrapped in chains they still had no idea existed.

The Soviets had a system in place to track American dollars being spent in Russia, cataloging Serial Numbers on every single dollar that came through their hands.

It took time, all tracking and data input by hand, but Peter's father was given a list of the Serial Numbers, and a value of how much had been taken or destroyed, and that number was staggering.

He met with the leaders of the Politburo and with Gorbachev himself. Russia was already burdened under the pressure of Military spending required to keep up with the United States.

This loss would be devastating. It wasn't like they could report this loss as insurance and claim it back from the United States.

The Soviets quietly leaked word to certain international contacts — vague offers of a reward, veiled suggestions, whispered implications of a vanished fortune, and a large reward for any information that brought back its return.

It was these tidbits of dropped information that began and grew these rumors to epic proportion over the years. And the numbers never got close to the actual amount that was to be transported that fateful night.

The group sat under the dazzling sun of Athens, surrounded by beauty and history, they understood the shape of their future: a life spent glancing over their shoulders, a life of new names and narrow escapes.

In the quiet hours before dawn, Peter sometimes caught himself staring at Ilya, memorizing the curve of her face, the sound of her laughter.

Mikael woke from uneasy dreams, heart racing, convinced the knock on the door was coming.

Taranov watched the city lights blink out one by one and thought, bitterly, of all the homes they could never have. They knew, someone would never stop searching.

The days had grown heavier, the kind where silence felt like pressure and even sunlight seemed to carry weight.

Peter sat on the edge of the bed, fingers twitching, eyes flicking to the door like it might open with answers. He couldn't stand it anymore. A few more days passed, thick with tension and unspoken dread.

Against Taranov's cautious advice, he decided to call an old friend — someone who lived near the airbase they'd fled almost a month earlier.

Ilya had pleaded softly that morning, fingers gripping Peter's sleeve. "Please, just wait one more day," she whispered, her eyes rimmed red from sleeplessness. But Peter had only kissed her forehead, murmuring, "One call, Lyubimaya. Just one." And she had let him go, though the weight in her chest felt like stone.

He asked Taranov to go with him to the payphone. It would just be a quick call, he promised. Nothing risky. Nothing that would draw attention.

They slipped out of the small apartment they'd been renting, moving quietly through the square. The morning air was crisp, the sky a brilliant blue over the sunlit marble, but neither of them noticed. Every step felt heavier than the last.

As they neared the payphone, Taranov casually reached out, his fingers brushing Peter's arm — a small, almost imperceptible signal. But Peter knew immediately.

Taranov had lived too many years in shadows not to feel them moving. Something was wrong. Not loud, not clear — just... off.

A silence where there should be noise. A man watching without looking. A rhythm broken.

Peter's breath hitched. His eyes scanned left, then right, absorbing details in an instant: the man with a newspaper who hadn't turned a page in five minutes; the cigarette smoke curling from the alley without a visible smoker; the faint reflection in the café window, two men rising at once.

They casually scanned the square. Taranov's trained eye picked up on things most people would miss.

The man in the dark suit sitting at the café across the street — no one wore a suit in this part of town.

The gleaming new car half a block down, engine idling, facing the phone booth.

The two men standing too close to the phone, one of them lifting the receiver just as Peter and Taranov rounded the corner.

Taranov murmured under his breath, "Follow me."

They slipped into the narrow shop next to the fish stand, the sharp scent of spices and sea air wrapping around them.

They pushed through the aisles to the back storage room just as the commotion erupted outside — a sudden sharp clatter of footsteps, shouted words, the unmistakable sound of a chase igniting.

Without hesitation, Taranov shoved open the back door, sprinting into the alley. Peter was right behind him.

They ran.

Down the tight, twisting alleys, past laundry lines strung between balconies, through the clusters of tourists and locals, dodging crates and market stalls.

At first, they tried to move carefully, slipping between people, but as the commotion closed in behind them, their movements turned urgent, then desperate.

Peter's chest burned; lungs raw with every breath. His shoes slapped against cobblestones slick with morning dew.

Taranov barked directions over his shoulder — "Left! Right! Watch the stairs!" — his voice a razor through the chaos.

Behind them, the thud of boots on stone, the harsh bark of orders in a language Peter barely heard over the roar of his pulse.

They darted into the square, the sun blazing down on the white stone. But instead of crossing directly toward their apartment, they stayed to the edges, circling, doubling back, twisting through side streets. Right, then left, then right again — trying to shake the shadows that clung stubbornly to their heels.

More than once, they thought they had lost them. But every time, a noise behind them — a shout, the scrape of hurried footsteps — shattered that hope.

They didn't dare look back.

They just ran.

The circle widened, pulling them farther and farther from home, until they found themselves at the base of the Acropolis, staring up at the steep hill and the dead-end path ahead. Peter's heart dropped. They were boxed in.

He spun toward Taranov, panic flaring in his eyes. "Up?" Peter gasped. Taranov's jaw clenched. "Up," he confirmed grimly. And they scrambled, lungs screaming, up the worn stone steps, the world narrowing to sunlight, sweat, and the pounding of their feet.

Back at the apartment, Ilya had watched them leave with a knot in her stomach. She hadn't said anything — hadn't wanted to seem paranoid — but something had felt wrong all morning. And when the sun dipped low and they still hadn't returned, her fears hardened into certainty.

She and Mikael sat in the apartment, the bags packed, the windows darkened, the money hidden in false compartments.

As night fell, Mikael slipped out into the city, moving quietly through the markets, grabbing essentials, trying to listen without drawing attention.

Every face seemed too familiar. Every voice sounded like a whisper meant for someone else's ears. Mikael's hands shook as he paid the vendor for bread, his pulse hammering in his neck.

The sharp-eyed woman at the stall held his gaze just a second too long — or maybe it was his own guilt painting suspicion on every face.

He was sure he was being followed — or maybe it was just his nerves unraveling. But every face in the crowd seemed to linger a second too long, every shuffle of feet felt like a hunter on his trail.

When he returned, he was shaking. His voice broke as he spoke. "They're gone. Something happened. And we… we're next."

He collapsed into the chair across from Ilya, his composure cracking. This wasn't how it was supposed to end. They were supposed to be on a beach somewhere, sipping drinks under an umbrella, laughing about the old days.

Instead, it was just him and Ilya now — and they were out of time.

Ilya buried her face in her hands, fingers trembling.

The room around her blurred — the chipped table, the threadbare rug, the walls they had pretended were home.

She had imagined a thousand endings, but none like this: waiting in a dark room, counting heartbeats, willing a door not to open.

They talked late into the night, their voices raw, going in circles. Where to go? How long to wait? What if Peter and Taranov didn't come back?

But even as they argued, Ilya felt the truth tightening inside her chest.

She remembered the way Peter's voice softened when he read aloud from a worn poetry book, the one he'd insisted on packing even when they had to leave everything behind. She wept thinking she would never hear that voice again.

She knew Peter was gone.

She hadn't wanted to admit it. Hadn't wanted to face the quiet, gnawing dread that had lived in her heart since they'd left that morning.

But now, staring across the room at Mikael — pale, exhausted, his eyes sunken with worry — she felt the last pieces fall into place.

They had to run.

She fell asleep in the early hours, still wearing the sweater she'd pulled around her shoulders, curled on the edge of the bed like a child bracing against a storm.

When she opened her eyes, the light was cold and gray. Mikael sat across from her, the untouched bottle of vodka on the table, his face heavy with sleeplessness.

"We have to go," he said softly, his voice rasping like sandpaper. "We have to get as far away from here as possible. Now."

Ilya felt her heart stutter in her chest. She reached slowly for the sweater, pulling it tight around her.

For a heartbeat, she clung to the desperate hope that maybe, just maybe, Peter would walk through the door.

But deep down, she knew.

Peter was gone.

And if they didn't leave now, they would be next.

Her lips parted, a silent prayer slipping between her teeth, words she hadn't spoken since childhood.

Across from her, Mikael rose slowly, gathering the passports, his hands trembling. And somewhere deep inside, Ilya felt the last thread of her old life snap.

Chapter Twelve

Falling Forward

Their plan, like every plan, was simple on paper: travel by train and bus to Istanbul, then by train to Ankara, and from there — disappear.

They caught the early morning train out of Athens Station heading toward Thessaloniki Monastiriou where they had to change to a 9-hour bus ride across the border, through Tekirdağ in Turkey and down the coastline to Istanbul. Finally arriving in Istanbul's Esenler Otugari in the late afternoon.

The sun was setting and it seemed the shadows travelled with them.

They had a small layover until their next train left for Ankara, and they quietly sat at a small café, drinking coffee, not even feeling hungry although neither had eaten all day.

When they finally left, the train windows blurred with passing fields, the aisle echoed with foreign voices, and every station brought the same tight knot in their stomachs.

Would this be the place where it ended? They tried to catch moments of sleep in shifts, tried to eat something without appetite, and sat motionless like ghosts wrapped in borrowed clothes as the train continued bringing them further and further from the sea.

There were no light moments, no laughter, no breath of real relief. They carried the weight of those they had lost — Peter, Taranov.

The plan, so carefully laid out in the haze of late-night strategy, had never accounted for reality.

Ilya sometimes caught herself tracing Peter's name into the fogged glass of train windows, fingers trembling before she wiped it away.

Mikael kept his jacket zipped tight even in the warm car, as if the weight inside it — the small pouch of emergency cash, the passports — could somehow hold his spine upright.

Peter, for all his charm and brilliance, had never imagined they might fail.

He hadn't believed the Soviets would refuse the illusion, that they wouldn't buy the story of the vanished plane, the vaporized fortune.

In his mind, every contingency had been covered — except the one that mattered most: that the world would not play by his rules.

Mikael and Ilya were different. They never pretended to be smarter than they were.

They were young, suddenly rich beyond their wildest imaginings — and soon to learn that not a single penny of it could be safely spent.

In Ankara, leaving the Ankara Gari train station they drifted toward Gazi Universitesi, a bustling district full of shops, cafés, and university students.

It was alive with chatter and movement, and for a few days they allowed themselves the smallest comfort of anonymity, finding a small apartment off Ahuduhu St.

Mikael bought a Turkish-English dictionary, poring over words and phrases, hoping to close the gap of language.

There was no Russian-Turkish version, and though his English was decent, every conversation felt like wading through deep water.

At night, Ilya whispered through half-dreams, murmuring fragments of Russian prayers she hadn't spoken in years.

Mikael sat at the window, watching the city lights glimmer and fade, and if there was a game at the University, they could hear the crowds cheering on their local Football team, wondering how much longer they could hold on to the illusion of safety.

They had money — more than they could ever need — but they touched none of the stolen American cash. They lived off what little they had brought from home, counting every lira they'd converted as if it were their last.

The apartment was modest. They bought simple groceries, and slipped in and out of cafés, blending as best they could.

But the days and months blurred together, and beneath every quiet morning was the unspoken ache: where were Peter and Taranov? What had happened?

Every passing day made the silence heavier.

Sometimes they sat in the cafés for hours, not speaking, just scanning the door. Mikael would lift his head at the sound of boots on pavement, only to lower it again.

Ilya's heart would skip at a familiar laugh from across the street, only to crumble when the face was wrong.

They would sit and watch the crowds, hoping against reason that Peter would emerge from the street, smiling, arms spread, with a new plan in hand.

As days turned to weeks and then months, the weight of truth settled deeper into their bones.

They would not be coming.

One morning, Ilya awoke to a quiet apartment.

No sound of Mikael boiling water in the kitchen, no shuffle of footsteps across the worn floorboards. The apartment was small — two rooms and a bathroom — and there was nowhere for him to be.

Ankara Esenboğa Airport
April 1991

The ticketing hall was bright with glass and metal — clean and quiet in the late morning lull. Most travelers moved like ghosts, slow and silent, dragging soft-wheeled luggage behind them.

Mikael stepped up to the kiosk counter, dressed simply —
neutral colors, unremarkable, forgettable.

He placed both of their passports on the counter. Two
Turkish entry stamps. No exit visas required. Round-trip
tickets to Frankfurt, leaving in two days.

"I'll be paying cash," he said quietly, in clean but practiced
English.

The woman behind the counter smiled politely. "Of course,
sir."

He handed her a banded stack of hundred-dollar bills —
crisp, cold, and smooth-edged like they had come straight
from the U.S. Mint.

The clerk accepted the bills with both hands. As per policy,
she peeled off two for validation and slid them into the bill-
verification scanner — a machine tucked behind the desk,
out of sight from customers.

It blinked once.

Scanned.

Then paused.

She glanced down at the small gray screen.

A six-digit code appeared. Then a second. Then the screen
flashed:
**"MANUAL CONFIRMATION REQUIRED — U.S.
SERIAL MATCH"**

Her brow furrowed.

She tapped the machine. Tried the other bill.

Same message.

She didn't panic. This happened sometimes — counterfeit notes, unusual batches, or customs watchlists. She calmly folded the rest of the bills into the drawer, locked it, and turned back with a smile.

"Just one moment, please."

Mikael's mouth twitched, but he nodded, with the best smile he could muster.

The clerk stepped into the back room.

Three floors below, in a tiled office near baggage screening, a Turkish anti-fraud analyst named Selin Kaya glanced at the alert code flashing across her monitor.

She clicked into the file.

Currency Flag:
Series 1985 | $100 USD
Serial: 3319-0672 | Matched to Interpol tracking bulletin |
Origin: Soviet intelligence channel (codename:
"FROSTVAULT")

Her stomach dropped.

Not a forgery.

A ping.

From *that* batch.

She tapped a line on the interface — flagged the transaction for silent review — then called it up the chain, exactly as the alert protocol dictated.

She had no idea what it meant.

But someone would.

Within 90 minutes, a Soviet commercial attaché at the embassy received an encrypted transmission:
Possible match — Ankara. FROSTVAULT SERIAL DETECTED.

He read it once.

Then reached for the red rotary phone that connected only to a secure line in Moscow.

Back at the counter, the clerk returned with a gentle smile.

"Thank you for your patience. Your booking is confirmed. Here are your tickets. Please arrive two hours early for customs."

Mikael accepted them with a tight smile.

He didn't notice the extra stamp she'd placed at the bottom corner — an internal routing mark, invisible to travelers but flagged in security logs.

"We're okay," he whispered to himself while his eyes never stopped scanning.

He was holding something in his hands that wouldn't need to be carried forever.

Two blocks away, a man in a dark suit answered a call in the back of a silent sedan. He listened. Wrote nothing down.

Then said only: "Track the flight manifest. Don't intercept. Not yet."

He hung up, and the car pulled away from the curb — slowly, as if time itself had already decided to follow.

Ilya's heart pounded as she sat up. She searched her memory — had Mikael mentioned going out? Had they spoken of it the night before? The memory of just another night in this nightmare slipped away like water through her fingers.

Panic crept in.

What would I do? Where would I go? The questions tumbled through her mind.

Before the tears could come, she heard them — familiar, heavy footfalls in the hallway, each step a solid, graceless thud.

When Mikael opened the door, he found Ilya pale and trembling.

He gave a crooked smile. "What were you worried about, Matushka?" he teased softly. "I just had to walk. I went to see where we might get tickets to West Germany. There we will be safe from the Soviets."

Ilya let out a shaky laugh, the sound breaking halfway through. She pressed a hand to her mouth, her chest tightening with the surge of relief and sorrow tangled together.

Ilya's face lit up briefly, a ray of hope cracking through the weight of grief. She caught herself, the pain of loss rushing back, but still — there it was: possibility.

"Are we really leaving?" she whispered.

The next day was a flurry of quiet preparation.

They still had enough personal money to carry them, and the stolen cash remained untouched. Peter and Taranov had mailed much of the fortune ahead to a post office box in Chicago — a brilliant piece of the plan, parcels of "collectibles" and "knick-knacks" sent from all over Europe, each one designed to slip under suspicion.

Chicago had always been their final destination point. From what they had heard it was a melting pot of people and cultures, and they would find safety.

Mikael bought the plane tickets in person at the Ankara airport: round-trip, Ankara to Frankfurt, and then they would have a shorter bus trip to Kaiserslautern in the Rheinland-Pfalz area of Germany.

The round-trip booking, Peter had always insisted, would raise fewer red flags. Mikael used some of the American money to pay for the tickets, booking and paying at the airport where it shouldn't have brought any attention at all, as everyone had to pay for their tickets here like this.

The soonest flight was four days away. It felt like an eternity.

Those four days passed in a strange limbo. Where the earlier weeks had been thick with dread, these days were laced with anticipation. They dared, just barely, to imagine a way out — a new life, far from the cold grip of the past.

Ilya packed and repacked the same small suitcase three times, folding and unfolding clothes with trembling fingers.

Mikael scribbled and burned a dozen versions of their cover story, practicing new names in front of the cracked bathroom mirror.

Chapter Thirteen

Ankara

Lyon, France — Interpol HQ
Financial Intelligence Division

Luc Moreau had a taste for order — and a nose for opportunity.

He stood at the broad window of his sixth-floor office, coffee cooling in his hand, watching a pigeon try and fail to land on a frozen drainpipe.

The ping came through at 12:47 p.m. local time. A priority alert tagged from the Turkish central banking system, routed through a confidential Soviet liaison network still active — unofficially — under the name **FROSTVAULT**.

He scanned the alert:

Currency match: $100 note, Serial Block 3319-0672
Flagged at: Esenboğa Airport, Ankara
Origin: Soviet economic asset loss (unconfirmed amount, black-budget funds)

He tapped the side of the screen thoughtfully.

"Almost missed you," he muttered.

He'd heard the whispers for years. A crash. A stolen fortune. A vault that no one was supposed to know existed. Every so often, a serial number surfaced — Singapore,

Riga, Dubrovnik. But never enough to triangulate. Never enough to *follow*.

Until now.

He clicked a series of internal forms. Pulled up Turkish travel logs. Manifest data. Two passengers. Russian origin. Fake names, but the pattern was there — the small jumps between cities, the quiet spending, the refusal to linger.

He picked up the phone and dialed Istanbul.

A voice on the other end answered in Turkish. Moreau responded in fluent, honeyed French.

"Send me the footage," he said. "Quietly. I don't want this elevated. Not yet."

He hung up and poured the coffee down the sink.

He didn't need a team.

He'd go himself.

Some people chased fugitives for justice.

Luc Moreau chased them for something else.

On the fourth morning, Mikael and Ilya rose early, neither having slept more than a few restless hours. They packed lightly, leaving behind nearly everything from Leningrad.

The cab ride to Esenboğa International Airport was quiet, the two of them pressed into their own thoughts.

But the moment they walked through the glass doors, Mikael felt it.

Something was wrong.

At the far end of the terminal, at the very ticket counter where he had purchased their tickets, stood two men in dark suits — no luggage, no carry-ons, no pretense.

The woman behind the counter glanced in their direction, a moment of nervous recognition in her eyes, before quickly looking down.

Mikael's stomach turned cold.

His mind snapped into focus — the way it had in childhood when his father's anger shifted the room, the way it had in the army when the first shot cracked the air. Get out. Now.

He scanned the terminal. More suits. Eight, ten — maybe more — scattered with calculated carelessness.

Without a word, he grabbed Ilya's arm, spun them both around, and strode straight back out the door they had just entered.

Their suitcases dropped to the curb as he shoved her into the same cab they had arrived in and threw the other bags containing the money in almost on top of her.

The cabbie hadn't even had time to pick up a new fare.

"Simdi, lutfen — git!" Mikael barked in what little Turkish he remembered; voice sharp with fear. Please, now! Go.

The driver didn't hesitate. The cab peeled away from the curb as five more men in dark suits spilled out of the airport, scanning the street.

Mikael didn't look back. Ilya had ducked down from view in the back seat, frozen, her breath shallow.

She squeezed her eyes shut, a silent scream caught in her throat, the taste of salt and metal at the back of her tongue.

The driver glanced into the rearview mirror, and not seeing Ilya, asked Mikael sitting in the front, "To where?" he asked in Turkish, then again in English.

Mikael's mind reeled. They had no backup plan. This had been it — the one chance. He squeezed his eyes shut, trying to push through the haze.

"Ankara Garı," he said at last — the central train station. They needed to get out, far away, and fast.

The train station was a swirl of motion — travelers, students, families, porters — a sea of noise and movement.

They stared up at the departures board, hearts pounding. No destination was safe; no plan was certain.

Mikael remembered Peter's late-night stories of Americans and how rampant they were in Europe; rumors of Americans in Germany, the possibility of anonymity in the larger cities. It was a thread — thin, fragile — but it was something.

They had to get to Germany. More and more Americans had to mean safety. It had to mean the Soviets would be fewer and fewer.

A train to Istanbul.

A boat to Italy.

And beyond that — maybe, just maybe — some semblance of freedom.

They bought their tickets with their own money, the last stroke of luck in a day that had nearly destroyed them. What they didn't know was that each dollar they spent lit a flare — and someone was watching the smoke.

A long list of bill numbers had been provided to Interpol, reported as an international theft, with "Dangerous, Armed Terrorists" listed as the criminal element.

Behind them, the black suits searched their abandoned luggage at the airport, finding nothing but clothes — the last remnants of their old lives.

Mikael and Ilya boarded the train with only what they could carry, slipping into the tide of travelers, two shadows chasing the promise of escape.

Chapter Fourteen

How could they have known?

How could they have found them. Mikael thought about the day he booked the tickets, he did nothing suspicious, he was friendly, the counter agent was friendly with no hint of question.

He used the American money to buy the tickets. Like a light switch going off in his head, "that had to be it," he thought, "could that be it?"

As the train lurched forward, Ilya pressed her forehead to the window, watching the city melt into countryside, and whispered softly under her breath — a single word in Russian. "Pozhalysta," Please?

The train to Istanbul was packed, a blur of faces, voices, and motion. Mikael and Ilya huddled near the window, their fingers laced tightly together, eyes fixed on the dark landscape rushing past.

The rhythmic clatter of wheels over tracks became a lullaby and a warning, the sound that lulled them into uneasy rest and reminded them that every mile forward was a mile away from home, from Peter, from the life they would never reclaim.

They didn't speak much on the journey.

There was nothing left to say.

Words had long since failed them. What was there to explain, when everything they were ran through the press of their hands, and the quiet exhale of shared survival?

From Istanbul, it was a maze of docks and back alleys, a scramble onto a boat bound for Naples, a night of huddled silence under a tangle of blankets, and then another train, another crossing, another carefully stitched escape.

The train rattled through the Italian countryside, its old wheels humming like a lullaby of metal and memory.

Night had swallowed the sky, and in the narrow compartment, the world outside was little more than shadows flitting past the window.

Ilya had drifted off, her head resting lightly on Mikael's shoulder, her breath slow, her fingers curled in the folds of his coat.

Sleep came in uneasy waves, shallow and strange. But then, in the deepest part of that dark silence, the dream found her.

She stood alone in a narrow corridor of stone, the walls slick and sweating, the air choked with heat and smoke. Her hands were bare, her clothes unfamiliar — a long white dress torn and scorched at the hem. Somewhere ahead, a light flickered — orange and low, dancing like candlelight. But when she moved toward it, the floor trembled beneath her.

Chains clinked.

Not from her wrists, not from her ankles — but everywhere. Dangling from the ceiling, coiled in the corners, threading through cracks in the stone like roots of fire. Every chain glowed faintly red, as if lit from within, as if forged from embers that refused to die.

She moved carefully; the echo of her footsteps swallowed almost immediately by the oppressive quiet.

Then she saw him.

Peter.

He stood at the end of the corridor, barefoot, shirt open, hair wild. Not older, not aged by time — just as he had been that last night in Leningrad, the spark in his eyes untouched. But his expression was not soft. Not warm. It was knowing.

"Ilya," he said, his voice echoing too loudly, as if the stone itself had spoken.

She reached toward him, but her fingers passed through flame. One of the chains curled like a serpent and snapped tight around her wrist. She gasped, not from pain, but from recognition — the fire didn't burn. It remembered.

"You're not free yet," Peter said.

She took a step closer. The corridor seemed to stretch, the light flickering brighter.

"I didn't leave you," she whispered, tears pricking her eyes. "I didn't abandon you."

*"You did what we all had to do," he said. But his eyes —
God, his eyes — they were filled with something she
couldn't name. Regret, perhaps. Or longing. Or the sorrow
of unfinished revolutions.*

The flames flared.

The chains began to tremble.

*Peter lifted his hand and the corridor shook. All around
her, links of fire snapped, broke, fell like dead stars to the
stone. But instead of collapsing, they burned there,
motionless.*

*"You think you're carrying the burden," he said, softly now.
"But it's not yours anymore."*

She took another step, closer than before.

"Then whose is it?" she asked, voice cracking.

*Peter's smile was sad, but whole. "You'll know when the
fire stops chasing you."*

*And then — he was gone. A gust of wind — no, breath —
swept down the corridor, extinguishing the light, pulling
her backward into the dark.*

Ilya woke with a start, Mikael shifting beside her.

The train clattered on. The sky outside was ink-black, and
the window beside her shimmered faintly, as if catching the
last ember of a dream.

She didn't speak.

But deep in her chest, she could still feel it — the press of heat, the weight of fire-forged chains, and Peter's voice like smoke in her ear.

You're not free yet.

In Naples, they crouched behind cargo crates as officials barked orders; in Munich, they traded a few of their last familiar coins for passage; they waited overnight in the train station, heads resting on their bundled coats, eyes open, always open.

By the time they reached Kaiserslautern, three days had passed, but they had been gone from Leningrad for months.

Months of fear.

Months of narrow escapes.

Months of carrying a weight they could no longer see as freedom.

Chicago was the destination Peter had chosen — the post office box, the final point in the plan, the landing place for all those carefully mailed parcels.

Kaiserslautern was a place Mikael had chosen, as just a way station along the way. He knew that he needed to find an odd job, and a small place to stay again. And he knew there were a lot of Americans here, and in his mind that might make it safer for them.

They arrived in winter, the cold a slap of reality after the long, drifting haze of their escape. Snow swept through the city streets, muffling the noise of traffic and people, layering everything in soft gray, inside, radiators hissed and windows steamed.

Mikael spoke English well enough to find work near the US bases in the area. They found a small apartment and life seemed to pass on.

But their existence would not be called "Life" to anyone else. For an outsider it would barely resemble life at all.

The experience at the airport in Ankara had left them both shaken, their nerves frayed with paranoia. They talked about it, questioning how anyone could have known, and Mikael kept coming back to his one thought – the money.

They were deathly afraid of spending a single dollar of it for fear of seeing ten more "Dark Suits" unexpectedly.

Chapter Fifteen

Taranov's Last Watch

Snow crunched beneath Taranov's boots as he pushed through the tree line, breath steaming in sharp bursts.

The cold was unforgiving in the forests outside Pskov.

His coat, once sharp and pressed, now hung heavy with mud and sweat. The wound in his side clean through, from the firefight at the extraction point throbbed with each step.

He didn't look at it. He didn't have time for the luxury of pain. He had stitched it himself in the dark, gritting his teeth against the needle he'd sterilized over a lighter.

There had been no mirror, no antiseptic, only vodka and willpower. He hadn't screamed, though he'd come close. That was two nights ago.

The plan had unraveled fast. He and Peter had separated just outside the Acropolis, ducking through two different escape routes when the suits closed in.

Taranov never saw what happened to the boy. One second, they were running together, the next Peter was gone. He had waited, as long as he could.

Hidden in the stone shadows of Athens, circling back, listening. But there was no sign of Peter, only the buzz of radios, the rhythm of pursuit, the tightening noose of surveillance. So, he ran. Not out of fear. But because one of them had to get away.

For three weeks, Taranov threaded his way north, from port to port, hitching rides with truckers and sailors, forging papers when he had to, trading silence for favors.

He moved like a ghost, his training taking over, instinct rising like an old lover from the grave. It was almost comforting, slipping back into the man he had once been. Almost.

He dyed his hair, wore cheap tourist glasses, grew a rough beard in days.

On the ferry to Varna, a child had asked if he was a pirate. He had smiled. "Not anymore," he'd said, ruffling the boy's hair. It was the first time he'd smiled in days. He thought of Peter at this age, and then the heaviness settled back over him.

In Latvia, he found a doctor who owed him a debt from a long-ago job in East Berlin. The man said nothing as he cleaned the wound, stitched the flesh. Just poured vodka over the gauze and muttered, "God help you." Taranov grunted in reply. He didn't need God. He needed a quiet train to nowhere.

But by the time he reached the border near Pskov, the net had tightened. The Soviets knew something. Not everything, but enough. And Taranov, once the invisible hand behind so many quiet disappearances, now saw himself marked as a traitor.

He didn't try to cross the border. Instead, he dug in; an abandoned hunting lodge off a frozen river, a place once used by Party men to drink and laugh and shoot at deer while the world burned. Now it was just a shell with a roof, a fireplace, and walls that remembered better days.

He found a stash of firewood in the shed, half-rotted but usable.

In a drawer, he discovered a faded pack of cards and an unopened bottle of Georgian brandy. "Even ghosts leave offerings," he muttered, uncorking it with his knife.

The first night, he lit a fire and listened to the silence. No helicopters. No dogs. Not yet. He ate from a tin of beans, drank melted snow and brandy, and stared into the flames.

The second night, they came. He heard the snow crunch before he saw them. Two men, maybe three. Boots. Cautious steps. Not soldiers, they were too quiet. Not hunters. These were the ones who came for people like him. He didn't run.

He waited in the shadows of the lodge, his pistol already in hand, breath slow and deep. As the first man stepped through the door, Taranov pulled the trigger once, twice.

The silence shattered. A scream. Another burst of fire. A figure fell against the window, glass shattering inward like frozen rain. Then quiet.

He waited. Minutes stretched. A drip of blood trickled down the doorframe. No more movement. No voices.

When morning came, he buried the bodies beneath the snow, dragging them by their collars into the woods. He didn't know their names. Didn't need to. They were just shadows sent by larger shadows.

He left the lodge that night. It was burned behind him. The blaze lit the trees and painted the sky in orange regret. A message.

He walked until his legs gave out and then crawled another mile.

Somewhere along the way, he dropped the empty pistol. It had done its job. Now it was just extra weight.

By the time he reached Minsk, his body was failing. Fever came in waves. He moved slower, thinner, a man pulled loose from the thread of time.

One night, delirious, he saw Peter. In a dream or maybe just the edge of madness. Peter sat across from him at a table made of snow. *You made it further than I thought,* Peter said, smiling, eyes full of the old fire. Taranov tried to speak, but his voice was smoke.

"Don't carry it," Peter said. *"Let someone else."* Then he was gone. He woke in a hospital, white walls and quiet murmurs.

His ID said he was Andrei Sokolov, retired engineer.

A man with no history.

The nurse brought tea. She was kind. She asked no questions. She offered extra sugar.

She looked nothing like his mother, but once - he closed his eyes and pretended she was.

In time, he moved to a town no one cared about.

Lived above a shoe repair shop.

Grew a beard. Fed stray cats.

Read old war novels and never spoke of the fire.

He didn't know what became of the others.

And if he tried harder to find out, he might bring attention to those who might still be left.

Sometimes, at night, he'd light a candle and set it in the window.

Just in case someone was still looking.

Chapter Sixteen

Moreau

Lyon, France — Interpol Regional Liaison Office
May 1991

Luc Moreau didn't keep a cluttered office.
He believed in surfaces. Clean ones. You could see
reflection on a clear desk. You could see guilt in reflection.

He stood before a corkboard now, arms folded. The walls
behind him were bare. The room smelled faintly of coffee
and static.

On the board: twelve photos.
Four apartment complexes.
Two dead men.
One blurry frame of a woman boarding a ferry in Piraeus.

Red thread connected cities.
Athens. Ankara. Istanbul. Munich. Kaiserslautern.

Only two people appeared in more than one photo: a man
with a haunted jawline and a woman with quiet shoulders.
Neither one looked at the camera. Both looked like they
were listening for footsteps that hadn't yet come.

Moreau tapped his pencil against a stack of transaction
logs.

- A flagged $100 bill at an airport in Ankara
- A reported gas explosion with no official cause

- A tourist visa issued from a consulate that no longer existed

He circled one line and underlined a date.

March 1991 — Kaiserslautern — Western District Precinct — Holding entry: Mikhail Ivanov, Ilya Markov. No exit log.

He smiled faintly. No exit log meant something had yet to be written.

He liked unwritten things. They always tried to hide their own footprints.

He stepped to the window.

The sky over Lyon was blue-gray, perfect and empty.

Somewhere beneath it, they were still moving. Carefully. Slowly. Like people who knew the past wasn't done with them.

He picked up the phone but didn't dial.

Instead, he took a pushpin and placed it in the corkboard. Chicago. Not for any reason he could prove — not yet.

But there was always a next city.

Always a next lead.

On the shelf behind him, a single black binder rested between volumes of bank audit law and diplomatic extradition treaties.

The spine was unmarked.

The label inside read:

FROSTVAULT
Internal use only.
Watchlist initiated: December 1989

FROSTVAULT ENTRY #104
Case Officer: Luc Moreau
Date: 21 April 1991
**Notes: Discretionary – Personal Analysis, Not for
Distribution**

*I've reviewed the Ankara footage again. Frame 44 shows
her boarding the ferry. Hair tucked, glasses on, but it's her.
Same tension in the jawline. Same posture I saw in the
Kaiserslautern precinct photo—like a violin string before
the note.*

Ilya Markov.

*On file, she's a cipher: linguistics student, no prior record,
presumed compliant partner. But that's the version the
archives offer. The woman in the footage isn't compliant.
She's calculating. Controlled.*

*I've spent years chasing men like Ivanov and Taranov—
brutes with spreadsheets, smugglers with God complexes.
But she… she doesn't fit. She moves like someone who's
already survived the story.*

*I caught myself staring at a still frame for nearly five
minutes this morning. She's stepping off the dock. A gull
flies behind her. It looks almost staged, like propaganda for
the resistance.*

I don't like what that suggests about me.

*I requested a copy of the customs manifest from Athens.
She's not on it. Mikael is. Not her.*

*So, either she's vanished—or she wanted him to be seen
alone. That's choreography. That's a message.*

They've got something. Not just the money. Something else.

*I've requested new clearance to travel. Vienna first. Then
Chicago, if the flagged bill in transit connects.*

*I'm no longer just chasing ghosts.
I'm chasing something I don't understand.
And I'm not entirely sure I want to catch it.*

And beneath that, handwritten in pencil:

*Last seen: Kaiserslautern.
Status: Active.*

Luc closed the binder.
Then the window.
Then the lights.

He didn't need to find them tonight.

He just needed them to keep running.

Munich, 1991

The kettle whistled just as the snow started again.

Anna moved slowly—deliberately—her hand wrapping the
towel twice before lifting the kettle off the burner.

In the stillness of the flat, even the ceramic clink of the cup felt loud.

She sat by the window with the tea cradled between her palms, watching flurries stick to the tram lines outside.

It had been six days since she saw the photo, just a piece of a news article.

It was tucked into the bottom corner of an Interpol bulletin she had no right to see, forwarded from a defunct mailing list she hadn't unsubscribed from—an old connection, back when she translated intelligence summaries for a federal contractor.

She didn't even know why she clicked it. Some habit. Some itch.

The resolution was poor. The woman was hunched, caught mid-stride boarding a ferry in Piraeus. Her coat too large. Her hair tucked up. But Anna knew. She *knew*.

You don't forget the way someone walks when you've lived with them in silence.

She'd stared at the image for a long time. Not because it confirmed anything—but because it cracked something open.

Ilya.

She hadn't said that name out loud in nearly four years.

Anna had been nineteen when Peter's father approached her. One semester into her scholarship at the University in Leningrad. She was diligent. Quiet. From a respectable family. And she was told—formally, politely—that a student of interest from Moscow would be joining the linguistics cohort, and that Anna had been selected to room with her. *To keep a file.*

They never said "spy." They didn't need to.

Ilya had arrived with a shy smile and worn boots. She didn't talk much. She studied at odd hours. She folded her clothes neatly and used the kitchen like it was someone else's.

And Anna had watched. At first. She sent coded reports once a week—generalized notes about Ilya's schedule, visitors, grades. Harmless things. Or so she told herself.

But Ilya had a softness, and it wasn't weakness—it was something resilient. A warmth held close, like coals in a scarf.

By winter break, Anna stopped filing the reports. She couldn't do it. Not when Ilya cried quietly in the kitchen one night after a call with someone named Mikael.

Not when she caught her tucking an envelope into a book spine, holding her breath like she was afraid the walls might breathe it in.

Anna never asked questions. She never opened the envelope. She just turned off the hallway light and went back to bed.

She assumed they'd vanished together after the fire. After Athens. After the stories of the bank, the explosion, the flagged bill in Turkey. She had grieved them like ghosts. But Peter... he hadn't died.

Peter had been captured and pulled out of the situation in Athens. Not tortured. Not tried.

Contained.

His father had leveraged every thread he had left to keep the family name intact. And Peter... Peter had become a reluctant pawn. Not imprisoned—but pulled back into the fold. A "consultant," they said. A "civilian liaison."

No one used the word hostage, but Anna saw the chain in his eyes when he finally was able to speak with her.

Once every few months, he'd send a one-sentence note. A location. A question. A warning.

She never responded with anything direct. Just a second-class parcel to a post office in Basel. Sometimes just a receipt. Sometimes a clipping.

She didn't know who else he trusted. She suspected the answer was no one.

And now, staring at the pixelated curve of Ilya's shoulder in that photograph, Anna knew what she had to do.

The envelope was unmarked.

Inside it: a copy of the Turkish newspaper clipping, a coded note, and an old postcard—faded, bent, and once mailed to Peter during their university days. The front showed a winter street in Prague.

She held it above the candle for a long moment—her hand trembling—not sure if she wanted to burn it or send it.

Then she snuffed the candle and sealed the envelope.

For Ilya, she thought.
For Peter.
And maybe, just a little, for herself.

In the summer of 1987, Peter had been a gifted linguistics and political theory student from Leningrad State University.

He had earned **a** rare clearance to travel abroad **as** part of a "youth delegation" — meant to promote Soviet internationalism.

Luc, then in his late 20s, was attached to French intelligence as a junior officer monitoring the Soviet attendees under diplomatic cover.

Luc remembered him mostly by the way he asked questions.

Not the loud, self-important kind that dominated academic panels or youth forums where people sometimes just spoke to hear themselves speak. These were quieter, slower, as if each word had been smuggled out of a locked room.

The boy—Peter, his name was Peter—had asked about sovereignty during a panel on post-imperial identity. Luc had watched from the back row, pretending to take notes.

Peter's accent was delicate, his French too perfect to be natural. He must have practiced it obsessively, Luc thought. That was the kind of thing the Soviets valued—excellence that passed for ease.

They spoke twice. Once at a reception, over cheap wine
and stale cheese. The second time in a shadowed corner of
a riverside bookstall on the River Seine, where Peter had
wandered away from his delegation to look through banned
Russian translations.

He had wandered, but even then, his protector was never
more than 20-30 feet away. But this man never interfered,
only watched to ensure Peter's safety.

Luc had pretended it was a coincidence; to run into him in
this book store. Peter had pretended not to notice him at
first.

"You work for the embassy?" Peter finally asked.

Luc had smiled. "Sometimes."

"And the rest of the time?"

"I read," Luc said. "I listen."

Peter didn't laugh, but the corner of his mouth tilted. "Then
you'll understand when I say I don't want to go back."

Luc felt something twist in his chest. Not pity. Recognition.

He then glanced at Peter's guard, and Peter shrugged it off,
in French telling him that Taranov didn't speak French and
wouldn't care what they said anyway, only that he was
safe, and was returned to his Father in one piece.

He could have reported him. Could have tested Peter.
Could have offered a line, a channel, a path out. But
something in Peter's eyes warned him off—not fear, but

resolve. Like he was already walking a wire and didn't need Luc's hands to steady him.

Luc did nothing; just listened and then watched him disappear across the bridge, coat collar turned up, hair damp from the rain.

And he never saw him again.

Not until Leningrad was burned into a name on a list. Not until **FROSTVAULT.** Not until the girl.

[REDACTED] – REPUBLIQUE FRANÇAISE

Direction Générale de la Sécurité Extérieure (DGSE)

INTERNAL MEMORANDUM – EYES ONLY

Date : 12 Novembre 1967

Classification : SECRET RÉSERVÉ

Objet : Echange Culturel.– Délégation Soviétique. Rapport d'Observation

Lieu : Paris, 6e Arrondissement – Institut Culturel Rive Gauché

Identités Observées :

1. [REDACTED], Homme ≈ 24 ans. ressortissant soviétique, liaison assignée – Institut de Fhtologie Orientale, Universite d Etat de Leningrad

2. Pavel Sokolov (alias : **"Peter"** ▓▓▓▓▓▓ + 22 ans. ressortissant soviétique, étudiant en théorie politique et linguistique. Observé en dialogue non autorisé avec personnel civil étranger.

Observations :

- Sokolov c'est soustrait à plusieurs reprises aux activites de la délegation sans escorte.

- Sujet apercu en conversation prolongée avec [REDACTED] dans zones non surveillées (notamment qual Voltaire et rue de l Université).

- Aucup échange matériel direct observe : le sujet a récupéré du matériel littéraire interdit en traduction.

Note de l'ānalyste :

Bien qu'aucune tentative de recrutement ne soit confirmée. l e sujet présente une adaptabilite cogntiive elévée, des tendances rhetoriques anti-autoritaires, et' une autonomie inhabituelle au sein de la délegation. Recommandation : manquage du dossier Sokolov pour surveillance à long terme sous protocoles [REDACTED].

Rédigé par :

Agent Interne [L M.]

Section C – Bureau des Opérations Stratégiques

Chapter Seventeen

Kaiserslautern

As Winter passed into Spring and then the beginning of
Summer, they walked everywhere they could.

The public transportation in Germany was excellent. There
really was no reason to have or need an automobile.

The rhythm of life in Kaiserslautern, or K-Town as the
Americans called it, settled around Mikael and Ilya like a
warm, if unfamiliar, blanket.

In the mornings, the sounds of shopkeepers pulling up their
shutters and the bells of the Mainzer Tor bus echoed up
through the narrow street. The old city still bore its history
on every wall, every brick, every uneven stone underfoot.

The facades were marked with age, the corners rounded by
centuries, and yet the place hummed with modernity.

They lived in a modest apartment above a bakery, where
every morning the scent of fresh bread drifted upward,
waking them gently. Ilya would sometimes stand by the
window with a cup of coffee, watching the bakers unload
warm loaves from deep ovens and arrange them in the front
display.

The baker's wife, a stout woman with cheeks perpetually
flushed from heat and flour, would wave to her sometimes.
Ilya never waved back at first, but in time, she began to
smile. Then, one day, she waved.

Mikael found work at a repair shop owned by a Lebanese mechanic who spoke German with a heavy accent and used French curses when frustrated.

The shop, nestled on a corner near the American base, serviced everything from local delivery vans to old American muscle cars imported by homesick servicemen.

Mikael fixed radiators, rotated tires, replaced worn brakes. It was honest work. By lunchtime, his hands were always dark with grease, and when he walked home from the bus at the end of the day, Ilya would tease him about the smell.

In the evenings, they fell into small rituals. A stroll through the Fussgängerzone, the pedestrian district, where they could window shop without needing to speak to anyone.

Sometimes they stopped for a Currywurst, sharing it on a bench like two old friends with nothing but time.

Other nights, they walked to the Pfalztheater and stood across the street, just listening to the music drifting out during intermission. Ilya, always wrapped in her old green coat, would close her eyes and sway, just a little.

They bought vegetables from the Turkish grocer down the street, always fresh, always cheap. Ilya learned how to make lentil soup from a neighbor's suggestion, and they ate it often.

When she thanked the woman, she stumbled over her German. The woman smiled and answered in English. "We all start somewhere."

Some Sundays, they took the train into the countryside. The Palatinate Forest spread out like a dream beyond the city's edge, all shadow and green, its winding trails and half-forgotten castle ruins offering a kind of peace they hadn't known in years.

Once, at the top of an old hill fort, Ilya whispered, "This is the first place I've ever breathed deeply without fear."

There were moments when they almost forgot what they were hiding from.

The photo was just the beginning for Anna.

Anna didn't sleep the night she first saw it. The image from Piraeus wouldn't leave her—the slope of Ilya's shoulder, the too-large coat, the tension around the eyes.

By morning, she'd opened the archives. Not government ones—those were mostly closed to her now. But university records, passenger manifests, oblique references buried in diplomatic leaks.

She'd once helped a defector smuggle microfilm in a fake prayer book; she knew how to look sideways at the truth.

She searched for any transit out of Turkey during the four-day window following the image. There were no obvious departures to the U.S., but a cheap charter line had processed two non-Turkish nationals headed to Frankfurt via Istanbul. Round-trip booking. Paid in cash. American bills.

She flagged the rail routes. One booking stood out: a short train from Frankfurt to Kaiserslautern. Two passengers. No return trip.

She stared at the names. Obvious pseudonyms.
But the handwriting on the check-in log?
Ilya's.

She copied the log, marked the dates, and folded it carefully into a small brown envelope.

Peter would want to see it.

They hadn't spoken in over a year—not directly—but his last message had been clear:

"If you ever find them. Let me decide what to do."

She held the envelope to her chest a moment before sealing it.

Then she mailed it to the drop box in Basel.

Not because she trusted the system.
But because she still trusted him.

When Ilya took on part-time work folding laundry for a nearby pension, she came home one afternoon humming. She hadn't realized she'd done it until Mikael smiled and said, "You haven't hummed since Leningrad."

Life in K-Town wasn't happiness, not exactly. But it was something close to peace.

They began to blend in. The grocer asked about their weekend. The neighbors nodded in the stairwell. Even the children in the courtyard began to smile at them. They weren't a mystery anymore. Just another couple finding their way.

Still, some nights, the past returned. Mikael would wake in a sweat, gasping, visions of fire and falling planes in his head. Ilya would hold him, whispering Russian lullabies neither of them had heard since childhood.

But in the morning, there was always coffee. And fresh bread. And the train rumbling past, calling them back to a world that had, at least for now, made space for them.

K-Town became home not because they chose it, but because it let them stay. And in a life built on running, that was more than they'd ever dared hope for.

Kaiserslautern didn't announce itself. It whispered. Cobblestone streets that curved gently between red-brick facades, a skyline broken not by skyscrapers but by church steeples and shuttered windows.

The only exception to that being the Rathaus, the Town Hall at the center of the city and at 25 stories tall, was one of the tallest in all of Germany.

Each morning began with a church bell — soft, low, unhurried — and the sigh of buses pulling away from the Stiftsplatz, their doors wheezing like tired lungs.

To Mikael and Ilya, the city was a kindness disguised as forgetfulness. No one asked too many questions.

The butcher remembered your name after the third visit.

The old woman who swept the stairs hummed the same lullaby every Tuesday.

And the man at the kiosk who sold newspapers never once looked at them like outsiders, though their accents betrayed them the moment they spoke.

There were small freedoms here. The quiet joy of a market tomato still warm from the sun. The comfort of predictable trains, always on time. The thick, meaty smell of Bratwurst from the vendor who set up just outside the Hauptbahnhof — always at the same time, always with the same burned fingers and soft voice.

It wasn't a city of escape. It was a city of rest. A city that let you put down the weight for just long enough to remember what lightness felt like. And in that space — that careful, cautious space — Mikael and Ilya learned how to exhale again.

With the little money Mikael was making, they could save and had enough of their own money in Deutsche Marks to buy food and a few other necessities and not have to worry about arousing any suspicion.

They both picked up enough German to get by. They still sounded like foreigners, but they understood much more, and could survive here as long as needed.

And for moments, there was almost a sensation as close to happiness as either of them would let themselves feel.

In both their minds though, their final destination, where the bulk of the money was waiting was in the United States, and there they both thought they would be able to spend it, and not live in fear anymore. The long arms of the Soviet regime surely couldn't reach them even there.

They saved money bit by bit, literally in a can in the apartment. As the can filled, they could see a light at the end of their tunnel, they began planning for the next, and hopefully final phase of their journey.

Mikael stopped by a Travel Office off the Stiffplatz and was assured they could book his transportation when ready, with train service from the Kaiserslautern Bahnhof, Train Station, to Frankfurt and then the flight to Chicago direct.

It took five years and two months of saving and scrimping every Pfennig and D-Mark, but the day finally came.

Mikael told Ilya that they had enough for the tickets, and then some – enough extra to convert to American dollars when they arrived to help them get settled before picking up the rest of the money.

Kaiserslautern, Germany — 1997

The bell above the market door rang softly as Ilya stepped inside, pulling her scarf tighter against the wind. The air smelled of citrus and old stone, the floor still wet from morning mopping.

She moved quickly through the narrow aisles — lemons, onions, flour — everything memorized, routine now. Her hands moved with practiced ease.

She hadn't noticed the car across the street.

Didn't see the man watching through the fogged glass of the café window.

But Mikael did.

He stood beside the bakery across from the market, holding two steaming coffees. He had meant to surprise her. He hadn't meant to spot the car. Black. Windows tinted. Idle too long. Too clean.

The kind of clean that didn't belong in this part of the city.

Two men stood near the vehicle. Not locals — their haircuts were tight, their postures military. They spoke to no one, but their eyes moved constantly, sweeping corners, scanning exits.

Then a third figure stepped out from the café behind them.

Mikael's heart slammed against his ribs.

Older. His jaw more angular now, face slightly drawn. A coat buttoned high over his neck, a black scarf tucked neatly inside. He walked like he always had — head high, hands still, like he owned whatever ground he stepped on.

Mikael took a step backward, nearly stumbling over a metal rack of newspapers. He dropped one of the coffees, the paper cup crumpling with a hiss of steam on the cobblestones.

He faded into the alley beside the bakery, heart pounding.

From the shadows, he risked a glance back.

The men stood just outside the café, speaking to a vendor in heavily accented German. One of the men from the car leaned in and showed the vendor something — a photo, maybe. A black-and-white print, grainy.

Mikael didn't have to see the picture to guess it was probably one of them.

The man took the photo back. He said nothing. But the vendor nodded vaguely toward the market across the street.

Mikael turned, fast, sprinting through the alley, rounding two corners, breath ragged. He reached the back entrance of the market and burst through it, startling the old woman stocking dried goods.

He grabbed Ilya by the elbow just as she handed over her coins at the counter.

"We have to go," he whispered.

She didn't argue.

She didn't even ask.

They ducked out the back, groceries forgotten.

Across the street, the man stepped to the edge of the curb.

His eyes lingered on the market's front door, expression unreadable. Not hurried. Not surprised. Just… still.

His companions leaned closer. "Did we miss them?"

The man didn't answer. He just slipped his gloves back on.

"We keep looking," he said after a moment, his voice quiet.

"Why?" the other man asked. "If they don't want to be found—"

The man looked up at the gray sky, at the flakes beginning to fall in lazy spirals.

"Because some debts aren't paid in money," he said simply. "And some stories don't end where we think they do."

The man frowned. "You sure they're still here?"

The man's gaze shifted to the corner of the alley, the faintest ripple in a curtain high above the bakery.

"They're close," he murmured. "I can feel it."

The other man stepped back. "Orders?"

He slid his hands into his coat pockets.

"We give them space."

A long pause.

"But not forever."

He turned and walked away, the two men falling into step behind him.

Back in the alley, behind the curtains of the small upstairs apartment above the bakery, Mikael stood perfectly still, watching as the man disappeared into the fog.

Ilya stood behind him, silent.

Mikael didn't turn. Didn't blink.

Her voice was barely above a whisper. "Was that…?"

He nodded once.

And for a long time, neither of them spoke.

They knew it was time to leave this place.

Chapter Eighteen

Not the real Athens

That night, Ilya couldn't sleep.

She lay on her side in the narrow bed above the bakery, staring at the cracked plaster of the ceiling.

Mikael was beside her, his breathing steady but restless.

The shadows outside the window curled like fingers around the frame.

She kept seeing his face.

Not as it had been this afternoon — angular, worn, distant — but as it once was: laughing in the soft light of their Leningrad apartment, cigarette dancing between his fingers, coat draped carelessly over a kitchen chair, his voice threading through the room like a fire warming cold walls.

"You trust me, don't you?" he had asked her once, eyes shining.

She'd answered too quickly. "Of course."

Now, years later, the memory floated back like smoke — slow, clinging, bitter.

She fell asleep sometime just before dawn, and the dream found her quickly.

They were in Athens again.

Not the real Athens — this one was wrong. The sky burned amber. The Acropolis loomed impossibly close to their apartment window. The square below pulsed with light, but no one moved. No vendors. No children. No music.

Just a low hum, like breath held too long.

She stood barefoot in the kitchen. The radio played a Soviet waltz that shouldn't be there. The air smelled of oranges and blood.

She turned — and Peter was at the table, whole, calm, and smiling.

He was younger here. The lines of fear hadn't yet etched themselves around his mouth. He wore the same sweater he'd had the night of the heist. A chessboard sat in front of him, pieces halfway through a game.

"I thought you were dead," she said softly.

He raised an eyebrow. "So did I."

Outside, something cracked. Like gunfire. Or firewood splitting.

She stepped closer. "Why were you there today?"

Peter didn't answer. Instead, he gestured to the board. "You're in check."

She looked. Her king was cornered. The black queen sat poised to strike.

"I didn't come to hurt you," he said after a moment. "But not everyone I'm with feels the same."

"Then why follow us at all?"

Peter's expression softened. "Because you and Mikael are the only parts of my life that ever felt real. And real things don't let go."

He moved a piece — his knight.

The board shifted. The room darkened.

"You're not safe," he whispered. "Not yet."

She opened her mouth to ask what that meant — but he was gone.

The chair empty.

The room cold.

And the radio still playing, now warped and slow, like it was melting.

Ilya jerked awake.

The room was dark. The radiator hummed and creaked. Mikael stirred beside her, but didn't wake.

She rose and stepped to the window.

Outside, the snow was falling again — clean, soft, silent.

She pressed her hand to the cold glass and whispered Peter's name, unsure if it was a wish or a warning.

She didn't know what haunted her more — the thought that the old Peter might be gone forever…

…or the possibility that he wasn't.

The envelope sat on the counter, unopened.

After the incident yesterday, Mikael had gone to meet a contact who could get them into Chicago under new names. Ilya stayed behind — not out of fear.

Out of purpose.

She stood at the kitchen table, slowly tearing their old documents into thin, clean strips — names, stamps, signatures turned to ribbons of paper that no longer meant anything.

When she was done, she burned them in the sink. No ceremony. No emotion.

Just flame.

Then she opened the floorboard.

It was the place only she knew. Not even Mikael had known — a gap between the joists under the bedroom vent. There, wrapped in linen, was one thing she'd kept since Leningrad:

1. A small sealed envelope marked in her handwriting: **IF M. IS GONE. OPEN.**

She held the envelope a long time before placing it in her bag.

If it ever came to that, she would be the one to act.

She always had been.

They thought she stayed silent because she was afraid. But silence was how she *listened*. How she *watched*. How she *waited*.

She wasn't hiding anymore.

Later that day, when Mikael returned, tired and anxious, he found her at the table, calmly making tea.

He hesitated in the doorway.

"Are you alright?" he asked.

She poured the water. "Are we ever?"

A pause. Then, without looking at him:

"If they come… you run. I won't."

He stared at her. "Ilya—"

She looked up — the fire of 1989 in her eyes again.

"I mean it."

He nodded, slowly. Not in surrender. In understanding.

She was no longer the one being protected.

She was the anchor.

And the storm was almost here.

Chapter Nineteen

Chicago

Almost another lifetime ago, they sat in Gaspodin
Lebedev's Biotech class in Leningrad, counting the minutes
until they could walk to Peter's apartment in the
Petrodvortsovy District near the University and begin the
weekend with a glass of Vodka and a shared meal.

Now, they counted those seconds and minutes until it was
time to go once again.

They'd landed at O'Hare just before sunrise, the city still
wrapped in ice and early winter light. At baggage claim,
Mikael kept glancing over his shoulder, sure someone
would stop them, demand answers.

Ilya clutched the envelope with the address of the mailbox
like it was their final lifeline.

The train ride into the city felt endless.

The language around them blurred into a buzz of sound,
every word unfamiliar.

When they stepped out into the street, it was colder than
Leningrad ever felt — because this time, there was no
going home.

The first time they saw Lake Michigan, frozen and
glittering in the pale sun, Ilya let out a sound that was
almost a laugh — or maybe a sob — muffled into Mikael's

coat. He held her tightly, his own breath fogging between them, and for a moment they stood at the edge of the world they had chased across continents.

When they unlocked the box, they found what they feared and hoped for all at once: the money had made it.

And, a letter unmarked, but upon opening, they knew it had come from Taranov. It had no name on it, or address, but in reading the words, they knew he had escaped and was still alive – somewhere. The handwriting was tight, angular — unmistakably his. Just a few lines in Russian, nothing sentimental. And one line at the bottom that made Ilya drop to her knees with the weight of it: "Remember the balcony in Athens — trust no one but each other."

Standing in the small rented flat on the north side of the city, surrounded by the neatly packed boxes, Mikael and Ilya both felt the same quiet dread coil in their chests.

They had survived, but the question they both felt, unspoken – would they finally be free? And, there was no mention of Peter.

They unpacked slowly, their movements tentative, as if afraid to disturb the air. The boxes lined the wall in silent accusation, their presence louder than any words they might have spoken.

The apartment was modest — two rooms, a bathroom, peeling paint, thin walls — but it was theirs.

By day, they walked the neighborhood, tried to learn the city, casually popping in and out of local shops, practicing their English, watching the rhythm of American life unfold around them.

But the money sat untouched.

They could hear it, in a way — feel it humming through the floorboards, see it lurking in the corners of the room, a presence they couldn't shake.

They had crossed an ocean for this.

And now, they were still afraid to touch it.

"We could take just a little," Mikael said one night, almost too softly. "Enough for a car. For warmth."

Ilya didn't look up. "And the moment it's traced?"

"We'd be careful."

 She finally turned to him; eyes hollow. "We didn't come all this way to end up caught by a receipt."

Mikael sometimes found himself running numbers late into the night — how long they could live on their small savings, how far they could stretch it.

Ilya stood at the window for hours, watching the snow fall in slow, lazy spirals, her reflection pale and ghostlike in the glass.

At night, they lay side by side in the narrow bed, the city humming outside their window, the steam pipes rattling in the walls.

Sometimes, Ilya would turn toward Mikael, whispering half-dreamed memories of Peter, of Taranov, of the cold nights in Athens, of the stolen moments before everything collapsed.

Mikael would hold her hand and listen, his face turned toward the ceiling, the weight of it all pressing into his chest.

They had survived what none of them had thought possible.

They had outrun the past.

But the past had come with them, sewn into their pockets, folded into the corners of every room.

It came with them into the grocery store, where Mikael counted every coin. Into the café, where Ilya studied the faces around her, half-waiting for recognition. Into the quiet moments between them, when the question neither dared to ask hovered like breath in cold air: Was it worth it?

On a gray afternoon, Ilya sat at the window, watching the street below — children running, couples hurrying past, an old man walking his dog through the slush.

Beside her, Mikael sat with a book, though his eyes rarely moved across the page.

Neither spoke.

They didn't need to.

The silence between them had settled into something familiar — not cold, not hostile, just… resigned.

They were free. They were alive. And they were living with a fortune they could never spend, a future they could never fully step into.

The clock on the wall ticked softly, the only sound in the room besides their breaths.

A radiator clunked.

Downstairs, someone laughed — a sharp, bright sound that felt like it came from another world, a place they might once have belonged but no longer did.

Now, two detectives were about to cross that same threshold, stepping into the same invisible prison.

Different faces.

Different stories.

The same burden.

Mikael closed his book softly, glancing out the window. Ilya leaned her head against the glass, eyes half-closed, the city reflected in the pane.

They had made it here.

But the weight of that truth, was something they would carry forever.

Chapter Twenty

Time to Bring Them In

Later that night, alone in his apartment, Nardone stood by the window. Rain tapped against the glass, steady and cold.

His thoughts drifted, unbidden, to the one case that had haunted him the most — a young woman who had agreed to testify against her boyfriend, a trafficker with deep connections.

The DA promised protection. It never came. She was found three days later, dumped in an alley like trash.

It wasn't the blood, or the crime scene, or the useless press conference that broke him — it was the voicemail she left him, still on his phone for years after. Just three words:

"You promised me."

It had changed him. Hardened him. And now, faced with the chance to finally cut a clean line between justice and survival, he didn't feel guilt — only fatigue.

Sayers, walking home that night, paused at the curb and pulled out her phone. She opened a message thread to her brother, thumb hovering over the keys.

She typed: "Thinking of making a big move. Will explain soon." Then deleted it. She wasn't ready. Not yet.

Her apartment was quiet, her keys loud in the door. She took off her shoes, stood in the dark a moment longer than necessary, then moved to the window and looked out across the roofs of Old Slovenia.

Somewhere out there was the flat. Somewhere out there, everything was about to change.

The next morning, Nardone's phone buzzed with a number he hadn't seen in years. He answered.

A gravelly voice greeted him. "They're watching the building."

Nardone froze. "Who?"

"Unmarked van, same two guys, fourth day running. They're not cops."

He thanked the caller and hung up. No name was needed, Nardone would never forget that voice. It was enough. Someone else was circling. Someone who hadn't shown up on any official radar.

It was a good plan. Maybe even the best they had. But as the hours ticked down, the simplicity of it was already fading, just like every plan before it.

Somewhere in the back of her mind, Sayers thought about something she'd once read — that no plan survives first contact. And this one? This one was already on borrowed time.

That morning at the precinct, Nardone watched Sayers closely. "We walk away from this clean," he had said quietly the night before, "or we don't walk away at all."

It wasn't a threat. It wasn't even a warning. It was just the truth, laid bare.

What neither of them could have known was that, decades ago, across a sea and a lifetime away, Peter, Ilya, and Mikael had once sat over vodka-soaked nights and drawn up a plan almost identical.

They too had believed in clean lines and beautiful simplicity.

They too had believed they could thread the needle between danger and freedom.

But theory, as it so often does, had collided with reality.

Peter had whispered promises to Ilya in the dark, tracing escape routes on her skin.

Mikael had folded maps until the creases frayed, memorizing every backroad, every alley.

Taranov had polished his pistol, his face impassive, the unspoken anchor in a sea of wild hope.

They had all believed they were too smart, too careful, too lucky.

And now, decades later, Nardone and Sayers were walking into the same fire — whether they knew it or not.

If they were going to pull this off, it had to happen fast —
yesterday fast.

Nardone and Sayers had gone over the plan a dozen times:
get Mikael and Ilya out of the apartment, bring them in for
questioning, clear the building, remove the boxes, and stage
a furnace explosion that would take out most of the flat.

They'd leave just enough money behind to throw off the
trail, making it look like an accident — a tragic fluke that
destroyed the fortune before anyone could claim it.

Simple in theory. Brutal in practice.

They'd paced circles in the precinct parking lot earlier in
the night, murmuring through clenched jaws, scribbling
notes on napkins, their coffee cold and untouched on the
hood of the car.

Nardone's eyes had been bloodshot, Sayers' nails bitten
raw, and yet the glint between them was unmistakable —
the glint of people already halfway past the line they swore
they'd never cross.

They rang the downstairs buzzer, waited for the metallic
click of the lock, and climbed the worn staircase to the flat.

Mikael opened the door without surprise, his face pale but
calm, as if he'd been waiting for this moment to arrive, and
not even surprised that it was sometime after midnight.

When Nardone told them they needed to come to the
station for a few routine questions, Mikael almost looked
relieved.

Ilya gathered her coat in silence, her fingers brushing Mikael's for just an instant — a touch so brief it was almost invisible, but the grief behind it hit Nardone like a blow.

These were people at the end of their rope, and somewhere deep inside, Nardone felt the first twinge of something he didn't have time to name.

At the precinct, they split the pair up — Nardone with Mikael, Sayers with Ilya — leading them to separate interview rooms.

Neither detective pressed too hard.

They offered water, asked if they needed anything, left an officer nearby.

It was all a careful illusion — just enough attention to look official, just enough neglect to give them breathing room for what came next.

In the interview room with Ilya, when she saw the flicker of fear in the woman's eyes — not of jail, but of something worse — Eva felt that old wound pull tight in her chest.

Something bad is coming.
Something bigger than us.

She didn't know if she'd stop it.
She didn't know if she even wanted to anymore.

But she understood something Nardone had never said out loud: sometimes, the burden isn't what you carry.

It's what you're no longer willing to put down.

Chapter Twenty-One

The Fuse

Minutes later, Nardone and Sayers were back in the car, speeding toward the flat.

They parked in the alley, moving quickly, hearts hammering as they kicked in the back door and sprinted up the stairs.

Inside, the air was heavy, the walls closing in around them. This was it — no more rehearsals, no more theories. This was the point of no return.

The smell hit first — old wood, dust, faint traces of mildew. The apartment was cold, the kind of cold that seeped into your bones, made your breath cloud faintly in the air.

Nardone's heart thudded in his chest, the rhythm sharp and relentless.

Nardone dropped to his knees at the furnace, wrench in hand, eyes darting over the rusted connections.

Sayers moved to the boxes, pulling off lids, her breath catching in her throat as the contents spilled into view.

Stacks upon stacks of bills.

More money than she had ever seen in her life — more than she'd ever dreamed of seeing.

"Come on, back to the plan," she told herself; "place enough money on the windowsill to blow out into the street when the gas furnace goes. All the rest of the money into the duffel bags Nardone had brought, and get out of here alive."

Her throat went dry. She reached out, fingertips brushing the edges of the crisp banknotes. For a split second, the room fell away — the precinct, the badge, the weight of years spent scraping for justice in a city that never had enough.

What if? The thought bloomed like wildfire. What if this was the door they'd waited their whole lives to find?

She grabbed armfuls and piled them on the window ledge, fingers trembling, breath shallow.

Somewhere inside, the voice of reason was screaming — this is insane, this is criminal, this is the end of everything you've worked for — but the louder voice was the one whispering of escape, freedom, a life unburdened by rules.

They were on the clock.

They had minutes, maybe less, to set the scene and get out before suspicion crept back at the precinct. They knew that. But in truth, neither of them had any intention of returning.

Sayers crouched near the wall heater, adjusting the timing device.

Nardone stood by the window, scanning angles, rehearsing exit points in his head. The tools of betrayal laid out like evidence before the crime.

He didn't have to check her work.

She didn't need to ask his opinion.

Neither had done anything like this before, but had enough anti-explosive training over the years.

"Wiring's clean," she said, standing. "Timer's good. Fifteen-minute fuse from ignition."

"Two exit options," he replied. "East stairwell's better. Less exposure."

She nodded. No debate. No ego. Just agreement — fast, fluid, familiar.

He watched her as she moved through the shadows, checking details he hadn't mentioned. She was calm, methodical. Unshaken.

"I used to think you were too by-the-book for this," he said.

She gave a faint smirk. "And I used to think you'd never ask for help."

They locked eyes for a beat.

Neither flinched.

"Guess we're both full of surprises," he said.

"I don't want to lead," she told him, softly but firmly. "I just want to finish this beside someone who sees what I see."

"I do," he said. "Always did."

They turned back to their work — unspoken timing in every movement.

No speeches. No confessions.

Just two professionals executing a plan that would burn the past down behind them — and leave just enough cash to start again.

Together.

Nardone's mind spun through contingencies: how much gas was too much, how long before the old pipes gave way, how fast they could be halfway to nowhere by dawn.

He clenched his jaw, blinking sweat from his eyes, his body moving with the fluid desperation of a man whose soul was already negotiating with itself.

It was Sayers who heard it first — the faint click of a door downstairs, the unmistakable shuffle of footsteps in the hallway.

Her heart lurched.

She moved to the window, eyes darting down to the street. Nothing.

But from the second door downstairs came the soft creak of hinges, followed by low, familiar voices.

"Oh no," she breathed, the sound barely a thread of air. Her fingers gripped the window frame so tightly her knuckles went white.

Nardone's head snapped up, his pulse roaring in his ears. For a heartbeat, they both froze — the last still moment before the fall.

Sayers froze. "They're back," she whispered.

Nardone looked up sharply, his mind racing. Of all the details to overlook, all the variables to miss…

Sayers cracked the door open just enough to see the two women at the bottom of the stairs, looking upward, talking in voices she couldn't make out, but aware of something.

"The old women are downstairs," Sayers hissed to Nardone, her voice tight. "They weren't supposed to be home today."

Nardone's jaw clenched.

He thought hard, trying to trace back through the swirl of planning and distraction — what day was it? Tuesday? Thursday? Their usual senior center lunch, their weekly card game — his stomach dropped. He'd lost track.

"Shit," was all he managed to get out, sweat beading at his temple.

It no longer mattered what day it was supposed to be or where they were supposed to be.   They were home now.

And he and Sayers were about to potentially blow up the entire building with two civilians inside.

The plan was unraveling.

Nardone's fingers flew across the furnace, adjusting the timer, recalibrating the gas flow, his thoughts moving faster than his hands. Less gas. Shorter delay. Enough to spark a fire, blow out the windows upstairs, scatter the cash — but not enough to take the building down with it.

His chest heaved, a silent war raging behind his eyes.

"Damn it, damn it, damn it," he muttered under his breath, twisting valves with shaking hands.

The wrench slipped once, clanging against the floor, and for a heartbeat, Sayers thought he'd break — that he'd call the whole thing off, that the last thread of his conscience would snap. But then he steadied. And kept going.

He cursed under his breath, his chest tight. Every shortcut raised the risk of leaving evidence behind, of getting caught, of tipping their hand.

Killing two innocent women was not a line he could cross — not even now.

Sayers hovered at the window, her chest rising and falling, eyes flashing between the street, the money, and the door.

In that moment, she felt the full weight of it — the badge in her pocket, the life she was about to abandon, the thin line between them and the dark.

And still, she didn't move. She didn't stop him.

Downstairs, the faint murmur of voices floated up through the floorboards.

"Damn it," Nardone whispered, his voice raw.

He could feel the weight of it now — the point where desperation and conscience collided, where theory met the jagged edge of reality.

He worked faster.

The night was still, the air sharp with cold, as the explosion ripped through the upper flat.

The sound shattered the quiet street — a violent boom that sent a column of flame and smoke billowing into the sky. Windows shattered, the old brickwork shuddered, and a rain of debris scattered into the alley and onto the cracked pavement below.

For a heartbeat, the entire block seemed to hold its breath — and then, dogs barked in a sudden, frenzied chorus, lights blinked on behind curtains, a baby wailed somewhere down the street. Then the entire night exhaled in chaos.

Inside the alleyway, Nardone and Sayers crouched low, arms over their heads as the blast rolled out above them.

Dust and fragments rained down in a stinging cloud. The heat hit their backs in a sudden wave.

Sayers squeezed her eyes shut, a sharp cry tearing from her throat as brick chips skittered off her jacket.

Nardone felt the concussion rattle through his bones, a dull thud that rang in his teeth. For a moment, there was only the pounding of his pulse, the scrape of breath in his throat.

Then — silence, except for the dull crackle of flames and the distant wail of approaching sirens.

Nardone pulled Sayers to her feet. His heart hammered against his ribs, his lungs burned from the smoke, but his mind was already racing ahead.

There was no time to linger, no time to look back.

He met her wide, terrified gaze for the briefest moment. "Move," he rasped, voice raw from dust and adrenaline. She nodded, jaw clenched tight, and they ran.

They ducked into the next alley, pulling the heavy duffels behind them — bags packed tight with money, the weight of it almost staggering.

Nardone glanced over his shoulder. For a moment, they stood in the glow of their destruction, watching the burning flat. No going back.

In that instant, Sayers felt something unspool inside her — not relief, not triumph, but a raw, scraping grief she hadn't expected.

The person she'd been only hours ago was gone, buried under rubble and ash, and in her place stood… what? She wasn't sure. She wasn't sure she wanted to know.

Hours later, the slipped into a motel they'd rented for the night was — one of those off-brand places near the airport where no one asked for ID if you paid in cash and didn't bleed on the carpet.

Nardone had gone to get food. Or maybe he just needed air.

Sayers sat on the edge of the bed, the smell of bleach and something vaguely floral curling in her nostrils. The glow from the TV flickered across the far wall, muted.

She dialed the number from memory. No hesitation.

It rang once, twice.

Then: "Eva?"

Her brother's voice was warm, a little groggy. East Coast time — probably close to midnight.

She leaned back against the wall, let the quiet hold her a second.

"Hey, Matty," she said.

"You okay?"

That was always his first question. Not *how are you*, but *are you okay*. As if, with her job, anything better than *okay* was out of reach.

"Yeah. I just needed to hear your voice."

A pause.

"That's the kind of thing people say before they do something really stupid."

She smiled despite herself.

"I might be doing something," she said. "I don't know if it's stupid yet."

Matty exhaled softly. "Are you in trouble?"

"No. Not yet."

Then quieter: "But I think I'm standing right on the edge of it."

A long pause filled the line.

"I've been running this race for a long time," she continued. "Doing the right thing. Following the rules. Watching people get away with everything while we bleed trying to stop it."

She didn't mention Michelle Torres. Or the cold file drawers filled with lives cut short by broken promises.

She didn't have to.

Matty knew her silences better than anyone.

"What are you asking me, Evie?"

Sayers stared at the water stain on the ceiling.

"I guess... I just want to know that if I make a choice — a real one, one that doesn't follow the rules — someone in the world won't hate me for it."

There was a soft rustling on the other end, the sound of her brother sitting up.

"You think I give a damn about rules?" he said gently. "I care that you survive. That maybe, for once, you stop punishing yourself for being the only one who tries to fix a world that doesn't want to be fixed."

She blinked fast, her throat tightening.

"You've carried everything for everyone," he said. "If there's something — anything — that gives you a little peace, you take it. Screw what anyone else thinks."

Another silence.

Then, softly: "You've earned it."

Sayers closed her eyes. "Thanks," she said.

"Don't thank me," he replied. "Just call me again. After. Whatever it is."

She nodded, though he couldn't see it.

"I will."   The line went quiet as she ended the call.

She sat there for a long time after that, phone still in hand, the weight of her brother's words settling over her like a blanket — not heavy. Just enough to remind her she didn't have to be the hero this time.

Chapter Twenty-Two

Execution

07:24 a.m.
West Precinct, 4th Floor

Officer Keene rubbed sleep from his eyes and stared at the whiteboard. Twelve open cases. Four interview rooms in use. Two supposed to be empty.

He frowned.

Room 3 and 4 were still signed out under Nardone and Sayers' badge numbers.

Except—he hadn't seen either of them all morning.

He walked down the hall, slow at first, then faster as unease coiled in his gut. Both doors were closed. He knocked on Room 3.

"Detective?"

Silence.

He opened it.

Mikael sat calmly, hands folded, as if he were waiting for a train. He blinked once at the light but said nothing.

Keene frowned. "Uh… hang tight."

He crossed to Room 4. Same knock. Same silence. Same result.

Ilya glanced up, her expression unreadable.

Keene backed out slowly.

He returned to the squad room and flagged the desk sergeant.

"Hey, uh... how long have these two been in the box?"

Sergeant Munroe glanced up from his crossword. "What two?"

"The pair in 3 and 4. Russian nationals, I think. They've been here all night."

Munroe's brow furrowed. "They weren't logged through holding."

"Exactly," Keene said, lowering his voice. "They're not booked. No charges. No translator. And no one knows why they're here."

Munroe stood, the chair squeaking behind him.

"Where the hell are Nardone and Sayers?"

They checked the duty log. Nothing since 02:47 a.m.

Keene grabbed a clipboard. "That's six hours off-grid."

Dispatch confirmed their units hadn't been called out. No radio check-ins. No filed reports.

Nothing.

Munroe picked up the phone and started calling them in order.

No answer.

No answer.

Voicemail.

Keene leaned in. "So... what exactly are we doing with two foreign nationals locked in interview rooms with no paper trail and no detectives?"

Munroe didn't answer. His face had gone pale, jaw working behind tight lips.

He slammed the receiver down.

"Get the lieutenant."

07:51 a.m.

Lieutenant Branch stood in the open hallway between the interview rooms, flanked by two detectives and an ICE liaison whose presence had been hastily summoned.

"I want everything logged," Branch barked. "Get a translator down here now. Pull the internal footage. See who signed them in. And someone call Internal Affairs before this turns into a damn press conference."

Inside, Mikael sat silently, watching the shadows move under the door.

Ilya's fingers tapped the tabletop in a steady rhythm; eyes fixed on the floor.

No one had told them what they were being held for.
No one had asked them a single question in hours.
And now, the panic had started to rise.

Mikael leaned back, exhaled slowly.

He knew this feeling.

This wasn't bureaucracy.

This was a cover-up gone sideways.

08:14 a.m.

Footage from the building's back lot showed Nardone and Sayers leaving just after 3 a.m. — dressed in plain clothes, loading two unmarked duffels into a city cruiser.

They hadn't come back. They hadn't checked in.

Their phones were off.

"Do we have any idea where they went?" asked the lieutenant.

No one answered.

Behind them, the monitor showed a frozen frame of the cruiser pulling out of the alley. The timestamp blinked.

05:03:18

And counting.

Chapter Twenty-Three

No Way Back

When Nardone returned, they tried to eat a bite, but neither could. They watched the news and listened to a police scanner for any news on the evening's events.

There had been a message about a small apartment fire in Ol'Slo but nothing major, and no mention of Mikael and Ilya yet.

They slept for a few hours, or at least lay on the bed with the lights out, each lost in their own thoughts, but neither wanting to talk.

The airport terminal was busy but not frantic — late-night travelers, red-eye flights, the hum of quiet conversations over drinks.

They tried to move inconspicuously, eyes lowered, hearts still thundering in their chests.

They had their tickets — booked days earlier, back when the plan had still felt like something distant, something almost theoretical.

A flight to Istanbul, and the train to Ankara. It was another name from his past that seemed far enough away from everything and somewhere two people could go to disappear for a while, or until the dust settles.

A new beginning. Or so they told themselves.

Nardone leaned against the gate window, watching the orange glow of runway lights dance on the tarmac. His reflection in the glass startled him — pale, drawn, a stranger wearing his own face.

Sayers sat hunched in a chair nearby, fingers laced so tightly her knuckles had turned white.

Neither spoke. Neither had to. The silence between them was louder than words.

As they sat at the gate, Sayers could feel the shift settling between them — the sharp snap of adrenaline fading into the heavier weight of consequence.

They were free.

And they were trapped.

The money sat at their feet, zipped away in black duffels. It was enough to buy a new life a dozen times over — enough to vanish, to rebuild, to start again.

And yet, the first time Sayers looked down at it, really looked at it, her throat tightened.

It wasn't just money anymore.

It was weight. It was heat. It was a burden stitched into the lining of their lives, pressed into their hands and pockets, pulsing like a live wire.

She imagined the faces they'd left behind — the old women in the building, the officers at the precinct, the colleagues they'd never say goodbye to.

She wondered if she'd ever sleep through the night again without dreaming of ash and sirens.

Nardone sat beside her, his posture stiff, his eyes fixed on the windows beyond the glass.

"Are we doing the right thing?" she asked quietly.

He paused. When he finally spoke, his voice was rough. "Ask me in a year."

The words hit like a stone in water, rippling outward, unsettling something she couldn't name.

She turned her face away, blinking hard against the sting at the back of her eyes.

His eyes stayed on the window, on the blinking orange lights out on the tarmac.

"It's not about the money," he said finally, his voice low. "It never was."

Sayers turned toward him; her expression unreadable.

He kept talking — not to her exactly, more to the empty space between them.

"I gave everything to this job. Missed birthdays. Lost my marriage. Worked cases that ate me alive just to close them and move on to the next.

I thought if I just kept grinding it out, I'd retire with some dignity — maybe a captain's bar and a plaque on the wall."

He huffed a bitter laugh.

"But what did it really get me? A badge. A bad back. A drawer full of unsent apology letters."

He rubbed a hand over his face. "You wanna know the truth? I didn't do this for a new life.

I did it because the old one wasn't worth going back to."

The silence between them thickened, but she didn't speak. She didn't have to. There was too much truth in the air to cut with words.

Sayers looked at him out of the corner of her eye — his posture rigid, jaw clenched, the flicker of something dark still haunting the edge of his expression.

Sayers thought of that night at Danny's. The words left unsaid. The weight of what might've been.

It had been a Tuesday, cold and damp the way only Chicago could be in late March. Rain came down in diagonal sheets, slicing through streetlight haze.

They'd ducked into Danny's, the diner off 63rd, half out of habit, half out of the need to be somewhere no one would look for them.

They sat in the back booth. The one with the cracked red vinyl seat and the table that tilted just enough to make the salt shaker roll.

Sayers stirred her coffee too long. Nardone didn't touch his.

"You ever think," Sayers started, then stopped.

Nardone raised an eyebrow but said nothing.

"You ever think maybe we just… got stuck? Somewhere along the way?" Sayers tried again, not looking up.

Nardone didn't answer immediately. He never did when it mattered. "We're not stuck," he said finally. "We're where we belong."

The waitress came and went. Neither touched their food.

"You ever wish things were different?" Sayers asked, softer this time.

The silence that followed wasn't awkward. It was fragile. *Like something might break if either of them moved.*

Nardone's eyes stayed on the rain outside. "Don't ask me that," he said.

Sayers nodded, and that was it. That was the night something could have changed. The night one of them might have reached across the table, said it out loud, done anything but leave it sitting there between them like a loaded gun.

But neither did. Not then.

They left separately. They didn't speak for three weeks after that. And when they did, the next case had already begun. The file dropped. The door shut. And whatever might have been — stayed where it was.

She wanted to ask more, to press beneath the surface of his words, but the silence that followed felt too sacred to disturb.

Thinking back to that moment, she realized she hadn't done this for the money.

She'd done it because she couldn't imagine walking back into that precinct without him. Because somewhere between stakeouts and late-night coffees, between shared silences and sharp glances that spoke more than words ever could — she had realized he was the only person who saw her completely.

And maybe he didn't love her, not in the way stories demanded. But he needed her.

And for someone like her — always strong, always guarded — that had been enough.

Around them, the airport moved on, the announcements crackling through speakers, travelers drifting toward their gates, wheels humming across the tiled floor.

For a moment, Sayers tried to imagine the future — Istanbul, the noise and chaos of the city, slipping into narrow streets, blending into the noise of another life.

But every time she reached for that image, something cold pulled at her.

We can't spend it, she thought. Not really. Not without risking everything.

She wondered if Nardone was thinking the same.

She suspected he was.

A child giggled nearby, tugging at his mother's sleeve. A flight attendant smiled wearily as she wheeled her bag past quickly.

The world spun on, indifferent, uncaring, and Sayers felt the sharp ache of knowing they would never quite belong to it again.

As boarding was called, they rose together, lifting the bags with quiet, practiced strength. The straps dug into their shoulders; the weight was punishing, but neither of them faltered.

They stepped onto the jet bridge like anyone else — two travelers bound for another country, another chapter, another chance.

They handed over their boarding passes, the scanner beeped and the agent murmured a polite "Have a good flight."

Sayers felt her stomach twist. It was done. There was no undoing it now.

As the line moved forward, they crossed that thin threshold between one life and the next, both of them felt it settle deeper in their bones.

They were leaving behind the world they knew.

They were carrying with them a fortune.

And they were walking into a life they could never truly live.

The burden was theirs now — not just the money, but the silence.

And it would follow them wherever they went.

Chapter Twenty-Four

They're Here

City Hall Press Room
Two days after the apartment explosion

The microphones were set in a crooked row on the podium;
each wrapped in the logos of local and national networks.
Channel 4. WCPN. WGN. A few freelance press tags
dangled like dog tags in the heat of the lights.

Acting Deputy Commissioner Frankel adjusted his tie and
cleared his throat.

"We want to begin by assuring the public that there is no
current threat to safety, and the incident on Halstead was an
isolated, tragic event."

He paused, reading from the page in front of him, but his
eyes kept flicking up toward the crowd — the kind of look
someone gives when they've been handed a story to tell,
but not the truth.

"At approximately 4:42 a.m., fire crews responded to a
residential explosion that leveled the upper flat of a four-
unit walk-up. Two tenants had reportedly vacated the unit
hours before the incident."

A reporter near the front raised a hand. "Was it arson?"

Frankel smiled — the tight, rehearsed kind.

"There is no evidence of criminal intent at this time.

Investigators believe the cause was a gas leak stemming from a faulty furnace.

We are cooperating fully with the fire marshal and utility company to ensure nothing like this happens again."

Another hand. "Is it true that weapons were found in the debris?"

Frankel blinked, just once, before his answer.

"There are conflicting reports. Debris fields are often chaotic. What we can say is that no live explosives were recovered, and there is no indication of a broader threat."

In the back, someone muttered, "That's not what the early scanner chatter said."

Another hand shot up. "What about the tenants? Mikael and Ilya... something? Why were they brought in?"

Frankel straightened. "Mr. and Mrs. — uh, the tenants — were brought in for questioning because of proximity to the scene and the potential for witness information. They were cooperative, and as of this morning..."

He looked straight at the cameras now.

"They have been cleared of suspicion and are being released."

Flashbulbs popped.

"Are they connected to the prior explosion in Old Slovenia?" a voice called out.

Frankel's smile didn't falter, but the pause between his sentences stretched half a beat too long.

"No further comment at this time."

Two blocks away, Ilya sat on a bench in the courthouse hallway, eyes closed, arms folded tightly around herself.

Mikael paced nearby, hands deep in his jacket pockets, jaw tight.

Outside, beyond the glass and stone, the murmurs were already growing. Reporters lining the courthouse steps. Microphones. Questions. Flashbulbs.

"They're here," Mikael said, not looking at her.

Ilya stood slowly.

She didn't ask who "they" were.

The press. The public. The ghosts. All of them.

When Nardone and Sayers never returned, with no one there to give a reason why they were being held at all, Mikael and Ilya were held for their safety, and then finally released, and for the first time in a long time, Mikael and Ilya felt the weight lift.

For years, the weight had been a constant — a shadow stitched into the fabric of every moment, every glance, every step.

As they walked out of the jail, down the main steps of the courthouse, Ilya looked past them and thought for sure she saw Peter.

And then, the reporters swarmed them both. Mikael put his arm around Ilya to protect her and she tried to shrug him off as she fought to find where she had seen him. There was no one there.

She struggled to see over and through the surrounding people, and she thought she caught someone ducking into the back of a car, wearing the same coat and hat that the man had been wearing.

Could she have imagined it, just as she dreamt of him and the chains of fire? No, she was awake, this wasn't a dream.

If Taranov had escaped and wished no ill will, then why couldn't Peter have gotten away and been looking over them as well?

She tried to tell Mikael, but the questions coming to him about the fire and the explosion at their apartment, one after another engulfed him.

She stood tall next to him gazing out, strong, and fearless to anyone looking, but really just hoping for one more glimpse of Peter.

Maybe she had just seen a vision, and maybe she had just seen what she had hoped all along for years.

She didn't mention it again to Mikael.

The crowd outside the courthouse was thinning.

Most of the reporters had gotten what they came for — the photos, the shouted questions, the non-answers.

The cameras were packing up. A few lingered, still murmuring about the explosion, the odd arrest, and the couple who walked out without a single charge filed.

No one noticed the man leaning against the far lamppost. Slim, clean-shaven, charcoal suit, a dark trench draped over one arm. Polished shoes, a gold watch that didn't quite match the local currency.

Luc Moreau watched them step down the courthouse stairs.

When he saw Ilya, something in her profile cut him. Not recognition, exactly. But resonance. Like seeing the shadow of someone you once failed.

He had seen her before, when he had first found out they were in Chicago.

The Art Institute had been quiet that morning — that particular midweek hush reserved for school groups and the unhurried. And most of the usual Art and Museum traffic was over at the new T-Rex exhibit at the Field Museum.

Light fell through the upper windows in long shafts, diffused by the high ceilings and pale stone. It was the kind of silence Luc Moreau had always respected — not empty, but observant.

He hadn't planned to follow her.

He'd been watching the building from across Michigan Avenue, a coffee growing cold in his hand, when the couple had arrived.

She wore a scarf — always the scarf — and the man, seemingly younger, carried himself with that careful anonymity Luc had seen a thousand times in fugitives. But it was her who caught him.

Now, standing at the far end of the gallery — just outside the American rooms — Luc saw her again, alone this time. She was gazing at a large oil painting. Something pastoral. Romantic. A woman near a river, perhaps. Luc didn't really see it. He saw her.

She wasn't watching the room. She wasn't checking reflections. She wasn't afraid.

She looked… sad. Not the fear-driven, hunted kind of sadness, but something deeper. The kind of grief that had finished blooming and was now just part of the landscape.

Luc took one step closer. Then stopped.

He could have taken her. She was right there. Call it in. Move fast. Close the case. He had the authority. The leverage. The face of a man who'd spent too long convincing others he was still in control.

But he didn't move.

Instead, he watched as she tilted her head slightly. Blinked. She reached up and touched the edge of the scarf near her temple — gently, like adjusting a thought. Her lips parted as if to say something, but there was no one to hear it.

And then, as if sensing him, she turned.

Not fully — just a shift in posture, the subtlest angle of awareness. Her eyes scanned the edge of the room. But she didn't see him.

Luc stepped back into shadow. Not fear. Not regret. Just… ache.

He left through a side exit. There would be another time.

And now, here she was again, and with the money gone, no reason for him to approach.

He saw Mikael, the younger man, with his arm gently shielding Ilya.
Ilya scanning the crowd — not nervously, but searching. Hopeful.

Moreau tilted his head slightly.

So. These were the ones.

He took a sip from a small paper coffee cup. Lukewarm. Terrible.

He didn't mind.

The rumors had led him from Lyon to Istanbul, then to a dead hotel registry in Frankfurt.

But it was the flagged serials — the bills in Ankara, now long buried under bureaucratic noise — that finally told him where to look.

And here they were once again.

He didn't move toward them. Didn't take out his phone.
Just watched.

If any of the money had survived, it would be traced and he
would find them.

He wasn't hunting now.

He was observing.

Gathering context, as he always told himself.

Mikael and Ilya disappeared into the crowd.
Moreau dropped his cup into a trash bin.
Then turned and walked away without a sound.

Behind him, the courthouse loomed like a tired monument
to order — too slow to stop anything that really mattered.

Chapter Twenty-Five

Burden Reassigned

Half a world away, in a rented flat tucked in the labyrinth streets of Istanbul, Nardone stood at a window much like Ilya's, watching a city that was both new and already heavy with routine.

Below, the market bustled, the call to prayer echoed through the narrow alleys, and Sayers moved around the apartment, unpacking the last of their few belongings, her motions tight, restless, distracted.

The duffels sat in the corner, zipped and silent. The hum of tension all around them, the fabric taut like a held breath.

The scent of strong Turkish coffee hung in the air, mingling with the faint tang of seawater and spice drifting through the open window.

Nardone's fingers tapped absently against the sill as he watched a boy chase a stray cat through the alley, laughter bouncing between the stone walls — a sound sharp with life, foreign to the quiet that pressed inside their flat.

Nardone ran a hand through his hair, feeling the tension settle deep in his chest.

They had escaped, but the weight of the money had only grown heavier in their hands.

It sat there, patient and unspent, a silent judge in the corner. He felt its presence in the pauses between their conversations, in the uneaten meals, in the way Sayers' eyes never quite met his anymore. They had crossed borders, but the border inside them had only grown sharper.

He turned from the window, watching Sayers move, feeling the unspoken words stretch between them.

There was no laughter here, no lightness.

Not yet.

Maybe not ever.

The burden that Mikael and Ilya had carried for so long had found new shoulders.

And so, the cycle turned.

Mikeal and Ilya returned to the apartment to find it burned out, and all their possessions gone. Small charred fragments of 100-dollar bills floated down, only causing them to smile and laugh like two crazy people once the realization hit them — the weight they carried was no longer theirs.

The neighbors stared at them from across the street, wide-eyed, as if expecting collapse or grief.

But instead, there they were — Mikael doubled over with laughter, Ilya's face wet with tears she could not explain, their arms thrown around each other in a mad, breathless embrace.

The cold wind whipped ash and soot through the empty windows, and still they laughed.

It was subtle at first — a softening around their shoulders, a lightness in the way they moved through the streets, pausing a second longer at the fruit market not worried about who they might see, or who might see them, the absence of the familiar knot in their stomachs when a stranger lingered too long near their door.

The money, once a towering presence in the corners of their small Chicago flat, had slowly become background noise. They had learned, at last, to let it fade — to let it rest, untouched, until it was little more than a memory folded into the past, and now forever gone.

Ilya was sitting downstairs, outside the flat, while construction workers who had been rebuilding there for weeks already, putting in new windows, redoing the electric, and basically completing the entire top floor of the flat.

A gentleman approached; he looked vaguely familiar, but Ilya couldn't place exactly where she had seen him, or recognized him from.

Ilya didn't look up when he sat across from her. She had known one day he would come. Maybe not today, maybe not here—but eventually.

Luc set his coat down beside him, hands flat on the table. No badge. No folder. No weapon.

He hadn't followed them directly. He had followed the parcels, the flagged serials. And every road eventually pointed here.

"You know I have nothing," he said.

Ilya's lips curled slightly. "That makes two of us."

The silence stretched.

"Interpol's moved on," Luc murmured. "No assets to seize. No warrants that would stick. No extradition partners interested in chasing ghosts."

"Is that what we are?" she asked.

Luc shrugged. "You more than me."

She poured tea from the pot that sat on the cheap patio table between them. No sugar. No cream. "You have followed us a long time."

"I thought there would be answers," he said. "Or at least resolution."

"There's only ever aftermath," Ilya said softly. "And memory."

Luc looked at her for a long moment. "Peter asked me not to follow you anymore."

That caught her. Her hand paused mid-air. Her eyes searched his.

"He said you'd done enough," Luc added. "That whatever you were running from, it wasn't his to chase anymore."

Ilya nodded once. Not slowly. Not sadly. Just… finished.

Luc stood, leaving the untouched cup.

"I hope you find something worth carrying," he said.

"I already did," she replied.

When he walked away, she didn't watch him go.

Over time, Mikael and Ilya found other routines: Ilya volunteering at a local bakery, Mikael helping a neighbor fix his car, small gestures that tethered them to the ordinary.

Ilya dusted flour off her apron; Mikeal wiped grease off his hands, both slowly feeling human again.

The streets grew familiar, the faces less sharp with threat, and the nights less crowded. For the first time in years, they began to sleep through till morning.

One morning, as the sun filtered through the curtains, Ilya stood at the window of the now new flat, watching the quiet pulse of the neighborhood below — the children darting past on their way to school, the shopkeepers unlocking their doors, the old man with his dog pausing at the lamppost.

Mikael brought her coffee, pressing it gently into her hands. She looked at him, slowly blinking her eyes and he felt her "Thank you," shared without saying a word.

The warmth of the mug seeped into her palms, and she closed her eyes briefly, breathing in the scent of coffee and soap and sunlit wood.

Mikael brushed a hand lightly against her shoulder as he passed, and she turned, resting her forehead against his, a quiet smile tugging at the corners of her mouth.

And for the first time in years, Mikael smiled back without the old fear in his eyes. The weight was gone.

Or rather — it was no longer theirs to carry.

Chapter Twenty-Six

The Burden

Internal Affairs Division — Case Review Office, 9th Precinct
two hours after the press conference

Detective Lila Moreno rubbed her thumb across the faded edge of the duty roster. She wasn't supposed to be working today — not officially. But the call from Lieutenant Branch had come with that voice, the one that said, "Just... look into it, will you?"

So, she did.

Room 3 and 4 had been signed out by Sayers and Nardone at 04:12 a.m.
Surveillance footage showed them leaving at 05:03 with unlogged duffels.
They hadn't returned.
They hadn't reported in.
And no one could find them.

And now, two foreign nationals who had never been processed, never booked, were being released after a four-alarm gas explosion conveniently destroyed their residence... with no cause of detention, no charges filed, and no one claiming authorship of the investigation.

Moreno exhaled slowly and sat back in her chair.

She clicked open a browser window on her terminal.

Incident: Old Slovenia — Pontiac Explosion — 6 Weeks Ago

She scanned quickly.

Gas tank rupture. No suspects. Three men dead. All IDs listed as "pending."

But a note in the report caught her eye:

"One of the deceased had a Russian Special Forces tattoo. Partial remains recovered from front seat."

Moreno's cursor hovered. She pulled up Nardone's case log.

He'd been lead on the Old Slovenia file.
And so had Sayers.
Both of them. Again.

A soft knock at the door broke her concentration. It was Keene — the patrol officer who'd first noticed the holding-room irregularity.

"You asked for anything weird in the logs?"

She nodded. "What've you got?"

Keene passed her a slip of yellow paper.

"Audio pulled from security feed. Room 3. Just before Nardone left with the male tenant. No transcript in the log."

Moreno squinted. "You have it?"

He hit play on his phone. The clip was scratchy, but one line came through clear — Nardone's voice, quiet but distinct.

"This is your one chance to walk out alive."

Then silence. Then footsteps.

Then the door shutting.

Keene looked at her. "That doesn't sound like a witness interview."

Moreno didn't respond right away.

She picked up a fresh case folder, dropped the audio file into a new directory, and wrote one word on the tab:

BURDEN.

Then she locked it in the bottom drawer of her desk.

"You think they're dirty?" Keene asked, voice low.

Moreno didn't look up.

"I think," she said softly, "we've only seen the first crack in the paint."

Chapter Twenty-Seven

Istanbul

Across the ocean, the breeze smelled of cardamom and sea salt. Somewhere nearby, a call to prayer rippled through the air, rising and falling like breath over stone.

Istanbul had greeted them like a fever dream — warm and layered, the kind of city that didn't sleep so much as change masks after dark.

Ferries moaned across the Bosphorus, their horns echoing through streets older than memory.

From their rented flat near the Galata district, the call to prayer rose like smoke through the cracked windows, drifting above the clang of hammers and the low murmur of the street markets below.

It was a city of walls — some carved by empires, others scrawled in fresh graffiti.

Cats threaded their way through alleys like silent sentinels, leaping from broken fountains to awnings with the entitlement of gods.

Children played in the courtyards of crumbling Ottoman-era houses, and old men argued over tea on folding chairs that creaked louder than their voices.

The city shimmered with contradiction: ancient stone beside neon signs, forgotten chapels beside booming nightclubs, veiled women passing teenage girls in tank tops and mirrored sunglasses.

At first, Nardone and Sayers could almost believe they were invisible here. The chaos protected them.

But invisibility came at a price — silence, restraint, the endless calculus of who might be watching.

Istanbul pulsed with a kind of brutal beauty — the kind only survivors understand. It was not safe. But it was alive.

Sayers sat at the café table, a worn stack of postcards beside her. She sipped her Turkish coffee slowly — the bottom thick with grounds — and flipped over the top card.

It was blank. Like the dozen before it.

She held the pen poised, ink trembling at the tip.

Dear—
She paused. Crossed it out.

She wasn't even sure who she was writing to anymore. Her brother, maybe. Or a version of herself she barely remembered.

Across the narrow street, boys chased a soccer ball through a dusty patch of gravel, laughing as they darted between the broken curb and a stack of old crates. Their shirts were too big, their shoes mismatched. They looked happy anyway.

Nardone sat two chairs away, his back to the breeze, a newspaper open but unread. He wasn't reading it for the news. Just for the habit of turning pages.

He looked older now.

The gray had taken over his beard. His shirts hung looser. His eyes tracked the ball as it bounced off a wall and skidded toward the alley. One of the boys gave a whoop and sprinted after it, bare feet slapping pavement.

Sayers wrote one word on the postcard:

"Still."

Not as in motionless. But as in *still here*.
Still breathing.
Still watching the world from the outside.

She set the card down, unfinished.

"We gave up everything to escape," she murmured, not looking at him. "And now we never go anywhere."

Nardone didn't answer right away.

He closed the paper gently, folded it with care, and set it beside his glass.

"Maybe that's what peace is," he said at last. "Staying still long enough to know no one's chasing."

Sayers smiled faintly. "That's one way to frame it."

A waiter passed, nodded at them. They nodded back.

Behind the boys, a cat stalked across a low roof.

Sunlight spilled over the cracked tile, golden and thin.

The duffels still sat in a wardrobe in their rented flat —
untouched, gathering dust.

Sometimes Sayers opened them, just to count. Not the bills.
The breaths she took before closing it again.

They'd spent from their own cash, of course. And through a
connection Nardone knew of, had been able to trade some
of the bills in exchange for Euros.

They needed food, new clothes, rent paid in cash. A
doctor's visit when Nardone's cough wouldn't go away.
But the rest? Still hidden. Still waiting.

For what, they didn't know.

They never opened all the bags. Not really.

Some burdens weren't meant to be spent — only survived.

Years later, no one would remember the explosion on
Halstead Street, or the fire a week later. The heist would
become just a smaller part of a rumor, swallowed by time,
incorrectly remembered in online forums and whispered
between retired agents who no longer knew what was true.

That night, long after the city had gone quiet, John found
Eva standing barefoot by the window, her hands wrapped
around a chipped coffee mug gone cold. She didn't speak
when he neared.

She just watched the lights of Istanbul flicker across the
Bosphorus, like stars that had fallen into the water and
never quite learned how to rise again.

He stepped beside her, close but not touching. For a moment, they stood like that — not as fugitives or survivors, but simply as what was left.

"Do you ever think about the night everything changed?" she asked, voice low.

"Every day," he said.

She nodded, and they fell into silence again.

"But not like before," he added. "Now... it doesn't chase me. It just walks beside me."

Outside, a ferry sounded its horn. Distant voices drifted through the air. The city, always restless, kept breathing.

Eva reached out, her fingers brushing his. "Then let it walk," she whispered.

They stood there, together in the dark, letting the past settle without needing to bury it.

Author's Note

Stories like this one are, at their heart, about people — about the choices they make, the weight they carry, and the cost of freedom when it's chased at any price.

As I wrote this novel, I found myself drawn again and again to the quiet spaces between the action: the moments of doubt, longing, and human connection that shape us far more than any dramatic twist.

My hope is that in the journey of these characters — whether they are running toward something or away from it — you've found a reflection of the universal tension between escape and belonging, and the truth that some burdens never fully leave us.

Thank you for reading, for walking alongside these characters, and for carrying their story with you beyond these pages. — DJ Lord